NO FRIENDS OF MINE

absolutely gripping suspense fiction

VANESSA GARBIN

THE BOOK FOLKS

Published by The Book Folks

London, 2023

This book is a work of fiction. Names, characters, businesses, organizations, places and events are either the product of the author's imagination or are used fictitiously. Any resemblance to actual persons, living or dead, events or locales is entirely coincidental. The spelling is Australian English.

ISBN 978-1-80462-061-8

www.thebookfolks.com

Also by Vanessa Garbin

WHAT WE DID LAST NIGHT
THE LIES I TOLD HIM
YOUR EVERY MOVE
THE STEPS WE TAKE
THEIR LITTLE SECRETS

Full details can be found at the back of this book.

www.thebookfolks.com

Prologue

It's dark down here. Darker than the night.

I can no longer hear the keening shriek of the gulls or the howling wind as it sends frothy waves crashing against the shore.

Every time I try to raise my head or attempt to shift my arms and legs, sand, wet and clumpy from the rainstorm, finds its way into my ears and my open mouth as I gasp and choke for breath.

I'm not sure how long I've got. The old tarpaulin he wrapped me in and the rusty sheet of corrugated iron he rested on top of my body has allowed some limited breathing space. But it hurts to breathe, and I'll probably run out of this damp earthy air soon.

I felt every thud of sand he shovelled over my shallow grave only moments ago and I was stupid enough to think that after he stopped at one hundred and sixty-five shovelfuls – I counted – I'd be able to feel the vibrations of his footsteps as he left then simply burst out of my grave like the undead and make my escape. But of course, one hundred and sixty-five shovelfuls of sand, wet sand that is, is much heavier than I expected, and the person responsible for putting me underground has either tiptoed away from my body or is simply standing around my grave in silence because I can't hear or feel their presence at all.

Maybe I shouldn't have played dead. Maybe I should have groaned aloud so that they could properly finish me off before they ordered him to bury me. Because I doubt anyone will find me in time, and if I'm going to die, I just want it over with as quickly as possible. As in, right now. Because lying here alone, bleeding from the head, with only my thoughts for company, is pure torture. It allows me to mull miserably over what went wrong.

Regrets? Oh yes. I have about a million regrets.

I regret not listening to my mum all those years ago when she told me not to get too close to 'that blonde girl with untrustworthy eyes' because Mum had a vibe about her. I should have trusted Mum's vibe.

I regret not being by Mum's side the night she took her last breath.

I regret not taking that trip with her to Broome after her first operation because I was paranoid my boyfriend, Lance, was going to cheat on me again while I was away.

I regret not meeting up with that sweet, green-eyed guy who invited me out for coffee last year, while Lance and I were on a break, because who knows?

I regret not taking the time to watch more sunrises and sunsets, to smell more roses or any flowers for that matter. I regret not taking that backpacking trip around Europe I'd always dreamed of doing. I regret not ordering that fancy $20 dessert the last time I ate out. I regret not quitting the waitressing job that I've grown to hate. I regret not doing something amazing with my life.

At what point did I decide to just give up on all the hopes and dreams I'd held tightly to since childhood?

Ten years ago, that's when.

Most of all, I regret returning to this cursed holiday house. Why, oh why did I come? I should have just ignored the WhatsApp invitation and blocked her number. How did she get my number anyway? I changed it after high school, after what happened. Oh well, I guess I'll never know.

Something tickles my ear, a thing with tiny legs, and inwardly I throw a fit. Outwardly though, I can barely wriggle in protest. Still, I must have managed to move a little because more cold, wet sand closes in around my ears and face. I squeeze my lids shut. There's nothing to see down here anyway. At least whatever tickled my ear has been smothered in sand.

I spit dirt out from my mouth and try to calm my racing heart without sucking all of the remaining oxygen into my lungs. It's tricky.

Now, where was I? Oh… that's right. Regrets.

If the weight of the earth wasn't crushing me right now, and if I was standing upright instead of lying on my back, this is the moment I'd hang my head in shame.

My biggest regret ever is doing what I did ten years ago on that moonlit beach.

Because if it weren't for that night, if I hadn't finally confessed my love to him, people wouldn't be dead and I wouldn't be here, wrapped up like a poor man's mummy… awaiting my last breath.

My heart aches and my eyes prickle with tears as I desperately try to picture his face, his beautiful smile. I can't believe it's been ten years. Time has made it difficult to remember his features and without a photo in front of me, his image morphs into someone unrecognisable and fades into blackness.

I'm all alone.

All I can do is pray that help is on its way.

Or that death comes mercifully quick.

1

My phone vibrates in my apron pocket. The boss doesn't like it when we, the waitstaff, carry our phones on us while we're working. It's a fair call seeing as all the younger workers would have them glued to their palms otherwise, but today my car broke down on my way here and I'm waiting on my boyfriend to get back to me about a ride home. Hopefully this text is from him.

All night, customers have been entering the restaurant dripping wet, rain drops glistening in their hair and on their faces. One elderly gent warned me that a hailstorm was coming, and to make sure that I drive safe in this 'hellish weather' tonight. At least driving won't be a problem of mine while my lemon of a car is out of order.

I didn't exactly have high hopes that Lance would come through for me – he's a budding game designer who of course loves to game as well and can get quite distracted at times – so I feel relieved that he's finally texted me back.

When I've made sure that all of my tables are sorted, I quickly dash off to the staff bathroom – a small unisex toilet cubicle which is found at the very back of the building at the end of a narrow, dark walkway that is shared by a neighbouring restaurant and smells in equal measures of cabbage and urine.

Breathing through my mouth, I enter then lock the door and sit on the lid of the surprisingly clean-looking toilet so that I can read Lance's message.

My heart takes a dive of disappointment when I see that Lance hasn't messaged at all. I double-check the message I sent earlier. He's read my text but hasn't bothered to respond. Weird. No, not weird. Typical is more like it. And I'm the biggest idiot for putting up with his crap. My mum used to say, 'fool me once, shame on you, fool me twice, shame on me'. This is exactly what is going on here. The name badge pinned to my waitress uniform should say 'Fool' not 'Marilyn'.

The message I received is via WhatsApp and from a number I don't recognise. Probably another scam.

As I click to open it, someone bangs on the door.

'Get out, I need the loo!'

'I'll be out soon,' I shout, annoyed. Can't I have a bloody minute to myself?

'Unless you want me shitting my pants, you'd better open up now, Maz.'

I hurriedly open the door as Jonny, the apprentice chef, barges past me, shoves me out and slams the door behind him.

Though my boss is probably looking for me, I take my time returning to the dining area along the offensive-smelling hallway, my eyes glued to my phone and my ears attempting to ignore the disturbing sounds coming from the staff toilet which will sadly no longer be clean.

But as I read and re-read the message, and double-check who sent it, making sure that my eyes aren't playing tricks on me, I freeze on the spot, my heart the only part of me racing.

No. Surely not. Why has she sent this? Why, after ten years of silence?

> *Hey guys,*
> *It's that time of year again.*

Spring is in the air and summer is just around the corner.
Time to head down to the holiday house and soak up some sun.
Weekend of November 21st.
All food and drinks supplied, as always.
I hope you can all come!
PS: partners welcome :)
Lizzie xx

'Oi, Marilyn, get off your phone and get out here, it's chaos,' shouts my boss, who is peering down the hallway at me, his forehead shining with sweat.

I shove my phone into my apron pocket and raise my palms in apology.

'Sorry. My car broke down and I'm trying to arrange for a–'

'One of us can give you a lift home, now get out there.' He shoos me towards the restaurant floor and disappears down the corridor calling for Jonny.

I'm one of the restaurant's best waitresses, always getting tips for my impeccable table service, but the rest of the evening is a nightmare of orders taken to incorrect customers, and a dropped plate shattered and sent red pasta sauce splattering up the white trousers of one of our regular patrons.

I simply cannot concentrate.

Lizzie hasn't hosted a holiday house gathering in ten years. Not since... not since, well... not since what happened during our high-school leavers' celebrations.

It chills me to the bone to think of returning there, to that massive house filled with polished jarrah floorboards and gleaming marble tiles, to the barren white beach stretching out on either side of it, to the eerie bushland out back, and to the vast Indian Ocean churning out front like a dark, angry mouth. I'll never forget the sound of Lizzie screaming that fateful night, and I'll never forget the guilt I felt, churning in my stomach. Or the total heartbreak that came after.

I'm not sure that I'll be able to go back there. I've worked hard at mentally suturing the deep wound in the flesh of my heart and I'm not sure I'd survive the pain of opening it up again.

And anyway, Lance and I are saving to travel around Europe. Well, right now it's just me doing all the saving – by day-working at a city cafe and by night waitressing here at a local Italian restaurant – while Lance works on the game he's designing. I'd love to see what he's come up with so far, but Lance tells me that sharing his design too early will kill his creativity mojo, so I don't hassle him about it anymore. But I have warned him that I'm not sure for how long my aching feet can handle these fourteen-hour days, to which Lance always responds with a promise that he's 'nearly there' and that he'll fly me first-class around the world once his game is a great success.

Lately though, I'm not so sure that I want to be stuck beside him on a plane, no matter how fine the champagne or how decadent the food served onboard. I think I've finally had enough of his lying, cheating ways, not to mention his laziness too. He always disappears on late-night drives so that he can get his 'creative juices flowing' while I'm left to deal with the housework after a long day on my feet. But I've only got myself to blame. It's time for me to break the cycle of dating terribly unreliable men. I've had my fair share over the years, but enough is enough.

Two hours later, after all the customers have gone, I'm untying my apron, my legs and feet throbbing, when I feel a tap on my shoulder. Honestly, if it's my boss wanting me to stack the chairs on all the tables I'm going to scream. None of the other waitstaff ever get asked to do the shitty jobs that I get roped into doing. Maybe I need to get better at saying no.

But when I spin around, expecting to see my boss's cranky face, I gasp and put a hand to my lips.

2

Lance stands there grinning, dressed in his good jeans and one of his nicer shirts, a collared one, his light brown hair damp from the rain.

'You came!'

I throw myself into my boyfriend's embrace, grateful for the security of his arms and forgetting for a moment that I'd ever second-guessed him. Lizzie's message has really shaken me up.

A group of chefs and waitstaff whistle at us but I ignore them and revel in the fact that my boyfriend came through for me, which means he must care.

'Of course I came,' he says, chuckling.

But something is off. I stiffen and raise my head from his neck.

'What's that smell?' I lower my voice so that the lingering staff don't hear. 'That's not my perfume.'

I take a small step back and his hands fall away from my waist.

'Why are you all dressed up?' I ask, hating the suspicion in my voice. This is exactly the kind of question *How to Keep Your Man from Cheating Again* warned me not to ask. But screw that book, I want answers.

He shakes his head.

'Bloody hell, Maz, I came all this way for you.' He turns and storms out of the restaurant and into the rain.

Great. I just know I'm going to be the subject of work gossip for the next twenty-four hours.

'You'd better hurry and catch him,' my boss says with a sympathetic smile, handing me my share of the tips, which is not as much as usual but to be expected.

Lance's car is still idling in the carpark, so I pocket the money my boss gave me and make a dash for it. Thankfully, the passenger door is unlocked, so I slide in. The car reeks of the perfume I smelled against his neck.

'Who's been in here?'

'Really, Marilyn? Are you really going to do this? I drive out here through the rain, and you accuse me of–'

'I haven't accused you of anything. But I can smell perfume that isn't mine. It's on your neck and it's in your car. You'd ask me the same thing if I came home drowning in another man's aftershave.'

He's silent for at least ten seconds, while he reverses and then drives out of the carpark and onto the main road. His silence is not a good sign. It usually means his brain is hard at work, trying to invent a scenario that never occurred. Something carefully crafted to make me feel especially guilty for accusing him.

'Just because I made that one mistake last year doesn't mean you can keep accusing me of cheating. You forgave me. You need to move on.'

Tears prickle my eyes. But I'm more upset at myself. I know I should have higher standards, that I should have left Lance last year when I found out he was cheating on me with one of his online gamer friends.

But he's all I have. We met just over a year ago and he supported me while my mum went through months of brutal medical treatment for her illness before she ultimately passed away. I have no siblings and I've never known my father. And I haven't spoken to my closest friends, the only friends I've ever really had, including Lizzie, in over ten years. Lance is my family. He's my friend too. He is pretty much my everything.

His warm hand slips around mine.

'I had a family dinner tonight. You must have forgotten because you're so busy working all the time.' He says this in a mildly accusatory manner. As though my working all the time is at the core of our relationship issues. This is the way Lance argues. No matter what we fight about, instead of taking any form of responsibility, he somehow makes it all my fault.

'So how do you explain the perfume?' I ask, hating the sound of my own voice.

The rain comes down harder against the car windows. Something pings against the bonnet and the roof of the car, followed by multiple hits of tiny balls of ice. That old gent was right about the hailstorm.

'It's hailing,' Lance says, as though I need to be made aware.

'The perfume?' I remind him.

He sighs.

'A bunch of my younger cousins needed a lift into town. Some of them have just turned eighteen and wanted to go clubbing.'

I nod and tug my hand away.

'So, are we good?' he asks, his hands on the wheel.

'Yeah,' I say. 'We're good.'

But we're far from good. I'm not sure who this 'family' is that he got together with. He doesn't have any younger cousins, or any cousins for that matter – he told me this when we first met. His parents died in a car accident when he was eighteen and he is an only child. It's something we bonded over back then, the fact that we are both quite lonely souls.

I glance down at my vibrating phone and see that multiple notifications have lit it up. My old friends have blown up my screen with WhatsApp messages. Someone has created a group chat. They must have all received the same invitation from Lizzie.

I open her message back up and zero in on the 'partners welcome' line at the bottom of the message.

There is no way I'm bringing Lance.

That is, *if* I go to this thing.

But seeing the names of my old friends pop up on my phone has got me feeling nostalgic. And as painful as it might be to return to the holiday house, it might just be exactly what I need.

Maybe if I fully process what happened that horrible weekend ten years ago and fess up to my friends my part in the lead up, instead of locking it away and pretending it never occurred, I might be able to rebuild the broken parts of me. Maybe then I'll be strong enough to part ways with Lance, to finally sever the strings of my dependence on him, of my reliance on the familiar.

I tap out a reply on the screen, my stomach fluttering at the idea of driving down to the holiday house and coming face to face with Lizzie and the other girls.

A tiny part of me is excited and hopeful that this trip will be the healing balm that we all need after such a traumatic time together ten years ago. But the larger part of me prickles with dread.

What if the trip tears open my wound and I'm forever unable to repair it?

Will my friends blame me for what happened after they learn the truth? Will they hate me for what I did?

My phone comes to life with 'Lizzie is typing...'

Blood pulses loud and hot in my ears while Lance prattles on about his fake night out with his 'cousins'. I wish he would just shut up. If I'm honest, I don't care anymore. He can go and be with whom he bloody well likes from now on. Because I'm done with his crap. And anyway, I've got more important things to worry about now.

Finally, after holding my breath for what seems like forever, a message from Lizzie appears in the group chat.

Yay, Maz, can't wait to see you!
It's been way too long.
If you have a partner please feel free
to bring him along.
I'd love to get to know him.
Partners are completely welcome.
Plenty of room xx

'What's wrong?' Lance asks, shifting his hazel eyes from the traffic and onto me for a split second before turning his gaze back onto the road. 'You look pale.'

'Nothing,' I say, shivering, as the hairs on the back of my neck stand on end.

But it's far from nothing. Lizzie's message is strange. Why does she want me to bring a partner so much? And her 'I'd love to get to know him' seems a bit much. I wonder what the others think about what she wrote, seeing as she didn't seem as enthusiastic about meeting their other halves.

If Lance and I weren't tiptoeing on shaky relationship grounds at the moment, I probably would bring him along to this holiday next month, just for security blanket purposes. I'd feel safer having him with me while I face my old high-school friends after not seeing them for so long. But, if things keep going the way they are, I get the feeling that Lance and I won't be together by the end of this week, let alone the month.

I sigh and reread Lizzie's original invitation to us all, and the entire thread of replies. Maybe I'm looking too deeply into all of this. I rest my head against the cool, passenger window. Rain has since replaced the hailstones, making the roads slick and shiny and casting a grey veil over the world. Everything seems so bleak in this moment.

But I'll never know the reason behind Lizzie's invitation unless I go. And I'm going to have to attend if I want to come clean about the guilt I've been carrying for so long. Only then can I wipe the slate clean, reset my life, and truly start living.

Truly start living... Imagine that. Just the idea of it fills my stomach with fluttery butterflies of hope, as well as a few of the nervous-wreak variety.

I squirm in my seat and stare out the window as houses and bus stops whizz by in a blur, unable to believe that it's really going to happen.

That after ten years, I'm finally returning to the place where the most tragic event of my life occurred.

3

The morning I'm supposed to depart for the weekend at Lizzie's holiday house, my car fails to start. I keep trying, turning the key over and over until the battery is dead.

Lance comes out, dressed in only a pair of boxers, showing off his newly sculpted abs thanks to his recent interest in going to the gym and working out. Although we've broken up, I've allowed him to continue to live with me in the spare bedroom until he finds his own accommodation.

After popping the bonnet and sticking his head under it for a while, he straightens his back and takes a huge bite out of the green apple in his hand. He meets my gaze and with his cheek bulging with fruit, he shakes his head.

'You're not going anywhere in this car,' he says, speaking with a mouth full of half-masticated apple. 'I think your starter motor has died.'

'Are you for real?' I groan and think about my neatly packed luggage stacked on the back seat, which includes some great new books I've been dying to read as well as several blocks of chocolate and a nice bottle of wine.

For the past week I've been so close to cancelling the trip, but last night, a strange sense of peace washed over me and calmed my nerves, and I started to look forward to a weekend with my old friends. I imagined all the laughs we would have over good food and wine, all the news we'd fill each other in on. The trip doesn't even have to be about what happened ten years ago if we don't want it to be. We are all grown women now. The past is in the past. Maybe we can have one last conversation about it and then put it all to rest, just like we put our friends' bodies to rest ten years ago.

But now, I'm beginning to wonder if my car not starting is a warning sign from the universe not to go. Either that, or the universe is telling me what I've known all along – that my car is an absolute pile of junk that needs to be scrapped.

'Sorry, bub,' Lance says, still using his favourite nickname for me. 'Looks like you're stuck here with me for the weekend.' He raises his brows suggestively.

'Don't even think about it,' I warn, quirking a single brow of my own. Lance has been pestering me to become his friend-with-benefits ever since we broke up.

My ex-boyfriend finishes his apple and tosses the core onto my flower patch.

'Free compost,' he says, grinning.

I shake my head but end up smiling. I can't be mad at Lance for too long. He is who he is.

'I guess I'll just get my stuff back out and unpack,' I say with a sigh. 'I doubt anyone can fix a starter motor on a Saturday morning.'

'If you had your manual licence, and not just your wimpy auto, you could've taken my car,' he says, shaking his head and tutting.

'Can't you be serious for once?'

'Okay, okay. I'm sorry, Maz.' Lance scratches the back of his neck and meets my gaze, his hazel eyes lighting up.

'How about this? I don't have any big plans this weekend.' He shrugs and takes a step closer toward me so that the single ray of sunshine piercing through the clouds beams a halo around his fair head. 'Why don't *I* drive you down to this… this holiday house? You said yourself that partners are welcome.'

'Yeah, but you're not my partner anymore. And anyway, what happened to that hot date you were bragging all week about?'

He waves away my suggestion of the date. 'I'm kind of bored of her already.' He grins cheekily and my heart can't help but still flutter at how handsome he is. 'Let's go as besties.' He shuffles to my side and elbows my arm gently. 'Come on, Maz, it'll be fun.' His face turns serious for a second. 'And it'll be good for you. I know you don't like talking about what happened in the past with your friends but seeing them again might be just what you need.' Lance hip-bumps me. 'And I'll be right by your side, for a shoulder to cry on or… for the laughs. Come on. It'll be fun, I promise.'

I gnaw on my bottom lip. He's got a point. It'll be good for me. Plus, now that Lance and I are housemates we do seem to have a lot more fun together. I'll probably feel a little more secure with him being there, seeing as the others are all bringing their partners. And Lance is great at small talk and livening up awkward conversations.

I throw my hands in the air and sigh in defeat. 'Okay, why not? But I'll be telling them that you're my friend only.'

'Fine by me,' he says, raising his palms. He does a little happy dance, rushes to get my bags out of my dead car and transfers them to his pride and joy, a little blue Subaru WRX.

'There,' he says, grinning. 'Now I don't have to worry about you driving down the highway on your own with this storm looming.' He points his two trigger fingers at me. 'How about you go make yourself a cuppa and chill on the couch while I take a quick shower and pack?'

'Sure. I might see if I can book my car in to get fixed on Monday. Highly unlikely but still worth a shot.'

Lance rolls his eyes. 'Um, considering how much old Matty loves you, I'm sure he'll manage to squeeze you in.'

I laugh and shake my head as Lance leaps over my rosemary garden hedge and runs into the house.

But my laughter soon dies as the dark clouds roll in from the west and obscure the last ray of sunshine. I say goodbye to any thoughts of sunbathing on the beach or dips in the ocean. Damn. Why are we getting so much rain this close to summer?

Thunder rumbles in the distance, low and ominous.

I'm not sure that I like the idea of the eight of us stuck inside the holiday house together for most of the weekend, but there's nothing I can do about that now. The best I can do is soothe myself with the knowledge that I can leave anytime I like if things get uncomfortable.

I nod, reassuring myself with that thought.

But as the wind suddenly picks up and goosebumps prickle my skin, I find myself wishing that I'd never agreed to this weekend getaway in the first place.

4

'In another couple hundred meters, there'll be a break in the trees, and you'll see what looks like a dirt track to your right. You turn down there. It's part gravel so your car will be fine.' I narrow my gaze and try my best to look for the little wooden sign through the heavy rainfall. 'I think it's coming up.'

'You *think* it's coming up?' Lance groans with frustration. He always gets cranky on long drives. I bet he regrets offering to come now. 'Why on earth did they build this holiday house in the middle of bloody woop-woop?'

A car overtakes us, a yellow Toyota Corolla. I remember seeing Tamara's profile picture on WhatsApp, it was a photo of her standing beside the exact same car. Up ahead it slows down and indicates right.

'Slow down. I think this is it. Follow the Corolla.'

Lance changes gears, swearing as they grind a little, then he slows the car down.

'This had better be it,' he says, turning the wipers on full blast. 'All this rain is pissing me off.'

Lance's grumpiness doesn't even bother me anymore because the sight of Tamara's car has lifted my spirits. Bugger the past. I can't believe I'm going to be seeing her again. I'm so excited. We used to be so close and had so much fun together throughout our high-school days.

Sometimes I try to remember how we all fell out of touch, but those days were so long ago and so hazy in my memory that I'm not even sure if it was me or the others who started ghosting first. But what I do remember is the fact that the pain following what happened seemed to ease somewhat once we fell out of touch. Sure, I've been living a meh life ever since, dating rubbish men and not exactly living the dream, but it's much better than the pain I initially felt. Now, however, I've come to realise that meh is not enough for me. I'm done with meh. I want a life. A good one. And if it means returning to the holiday house and reliving the pain and the trauma with my old friends, so be it. I'll get over it. I'll heal. I'll finally move forward.

'This is definitely it,' I say, giving Lance's shoulder a squeeze as we turn onto the track, the wet gravel crunching beneath the tyres.

'Oi,' Lance says. 'You said no to friends-with-benefits so my shoulder is off limits to you, Little Miss Touchy-Feely.'

'Oh shush.' I give his arm a playful slap and find myself grinning like an idiot.

Lance turns the wipers down one notch now that we're driving beneath the canopy of the enormous forest tree branches. With the rain slightly muted, I can hear the music playing on the stereo again. It's like we've entered a tunnel surrounded by nature, a tunnel that will magically transport me to my past, but also hopefully absolve me from it.

'You sound... and look a little happier.' Lance glances at me from out the corner of his eye. 'In fact, I don't think I've ever seen you like this... it's odd. Emo Maz is the only Maz I've ever known.'

'I do feel happier.' I take a deep breath and exhale as my eyes drink in the greenery that surrounds us. 'And I don't know why, but I have a feeling that this weekend is going to be... cathartic.'

Lance raises a single brow and looks at me before turning his gaze back to the gravel track, which seems to be filling with puddles the deeper we drive into the bush.

'You never told me what actually happened here all those years ago. You never trusted me with it, even though I told you what happened with my parents.' Lance keeps his eyes on the track but I can tell by the sudden rigidity of his body and the way he's pressed his lips together, that he's seriously upset by this.

'I know, and I appreciate that you told me about your parents. It means a lot. But–' I shrug and gnaw on my bottom lip '–I guess I don't like to talk about it because it's in the past and... it's difficult to talk about.'

'But I'm your boyfriend and...' Lance's voice trails off. 'Well, I *was* your boyfriend.' He sighs and his knuckles bulge as he grips the steering wheel tighter. 'But I guess what I'm trying to say is, that if you can't talk to me about it, I'm not sure if you're going to exactly feel comfortable seeing your friends again this weekend, after all this time. I mean, just seeing them is going to remind you of stuff... it'll all come flooding back.'

'I know that.' I don't mean for my words to come out so snappy, but they do. Lance is right. Here am I, feeling all peace and love and excitement after spotting Tamara's car, when the reality is, well... this reunion is going to hurt. A lot.

For a second the air inside the car thickens with tension, but then Lance looks at my face and rolls his eyes.

'Okay, okay, enough of the seriousness. I'll try not to ask you any more invasive questions.' He grins at me. 'This is meant to be a fun weekend.'

I smile with relief.

'Fun,' I say, trying out the word that has been a foreign concept in my life for the past ten years. To think that maybe after this weekend, when I finally put my past behind me, I might be able to move forward with my life and be happy.

'What are you thinking about?' Lance asks, a soft smile on his lips; but the smile dies as his eyes move back to the track ahead of us and he slams on the brakes.

'Lance!' I grip the passenger door handle with my left hand and push my right hand against the dashboard as we skid along the now muddy gravel and come to a stop only inches away from Tamara's yellow car.

Our bodies slam back against the car seats.

'You okay?' Lance asks, his left hand squeezing my arm.

I nod, my heart thundering against my chest, no different from the actual thunder rumbling outside.

'Oh great,' Lance says, when he spies the reason why Tamara stopped her car.

5

I sigh, staring at the large dip in the track, filled with brownish-grey water. The rain has formed a mini lake out here and with the massive trees bordering the entire track, there's no way around it other than through it. Unless we just turn around and go home.

'Do you think we can drive through it?'

'Only one way to find out,' Lance says, getting out of the car.

I get out, too, my stomach swirling with nerves. The rain has eased a little, but the fine sprinkles still manage to dampen my hair and clothes.

Four people get out of Tamara's car. Carpooling. Maybe the others have been keeping in touch all along and I've been the only one left out. Maybe they come here every year and this time Lizzie has decided to invite me along. My stomach swirls sickly. Oh God, why didn't I even consider that it might only be me that's been shunned from the group all this time?

For a second I think I've got it wrong, that the woman who's been driving isn't Tamara at all, but when she turns her head, long dark hair fanning out behind her, and fixes her pale blue eyes on me, I gasp. She's changed so much. Not just her hair and face, but her chest too.

Tamara used to be flat-chested all throughout high school. The boys used to tease her mercilessly, calling her 'ironing board' and 'plank.' But now she has massive boobs, so much so that the buttons on her shirt are bulging, giving us a sneak peek at her red bra underneath.

I elbow Lance in the ribs when I catch him staring and he shoots me a 'I can't help it' look. He's a self-confessed boob man. A month after we first met, he admitted that it was the first part of my body he'd noticed.

I can't believe that, after hearing me whinge throughout our high-school days about how annoying large breasts are, Tamara would go and get herself a pair of what look like size Fs. My back hurts just looking at them. But if they make her happy then good for her. I'm not one to talk. I've been considering a reduction in mine, which is still technically a form of cosmetic surgery, so each to their own.

A tall, thin, dark-haired man with a pirate-like black patch over his eye follows Tamara as she walks towards me, her pouty pink lips stretching into a wide smile.

She screams when she reaches me and engulfs me in a huge squishy hug.

I laugh and squeeze her back, my throat thickening with emotion. It's been too long.

Tamara draws back and lets me go to slip her arm around the tall man standing close behind her.

'This is my fiancé, One-Eyed Willy,' she says, giggling.

Her partner shakes his head but is smiling when he extends a hand to Lance.

'It's Jake, actually. I apologise for Tams in advance,' he says, rolling his eyes as he lets go of Lance's hand and shakes mine.

'I'm Marilyn. And this is my… boyfriend, Lance.'

Lance flicks me a quick glance before smiling at Jake and then Tamara. 'Great to meet you both.'

'Oh. My. God. Maz?'

Tamara and Jake part and a small, red-haired woman rushes through them and flings herself at me.

'Sienna? Oh my gosh, I love your hair,' I say, giving her a squeeze before stepping back to look her over. Same pretty, birdlike features, same glowing olive skin, only her old hair colour has been replaced with bright crimson. It suits her.

'This is my boyfriend, Lucas,' she says, taking the hand of a pale, blond man a head taller than her but still shorter than me.

'Hi,' he says, his cheeks flushing pink when our eyes meet before he casts his gaze to the ground.

Lance clears his throat and offers his hand to Lucas, who looks up and takes it, but when I go to do the same, Lucas takes a step back and turns to face the waterfilled dip in the track.

'Do you think we can get across it?' he asks nobody in particular. His voice is soft, feminine, and suits his pretty features.

The rain starts to fall heavier again, falling on us in patches through the breaks in the branches above. Lance snatches a nearby fallen branch from the ground and pokes it along the edge of the water. Then he quickly takes his shoes off, rolls up his jeans and wades in, stabbing at the murky body of water which has now come to life beneath the heavier rain. When he gets to the middle and stabs at it one final time, he turns around and grins at us all. The water only just reaches the bottom of his calf.

'Hallelujah! We can cross it. I don't know about getting back out of here, though.' He tosses the stick aside, his eyebrows dancing. 'The storm's supposed to get pretty wild tonight.'

Sienna wraps her arms around Lucas, who kisses the top of her head and strokes her back, like he's reassuring a frightened child. I can't deny they look cute together.

'Okay, let's go then,' says Tamara. She opens her car door then looks at Lance. 'Should I go slowly through it?'

Lance shrugs. 'I'm going to put my foot down, get through it as fast as possible.'

'I'd take it slow, Tams,' says Jake, who's eyeing Lance warily now. 'We don't know what's under that water. Could be branches, rocks… anything.'

When we get into the car, Lance grins at me, his hands on the wheel as he waits for Tamara to drive through the water first.

'Boyfriend, hey?' he says, his eyebrows still dancing. 'I'm looking forward to getting my boyfriend privileges later tonight when we're alone in the bedroom.'

'Oi,' I say, laughing and shaking my head. 'There'll be no privileges tonight or any night.'

'Then why did you say it? Hmmm? Me thinks you might still have some feelings for me, bub.' He looks at me and my heart softens at the hope sparkling in his hazel eyes.

Oh God, I need to be strong and resist his charms. This is what happened last time. Lance has a way of making you want to believe that he will never hurt you again. And I'm such a stupid sucker for him.

But not anymore.

'I don't know why I said it. Sorry. I think after hearing Tamara say fiancé… I don't know, maybe I felt a little…'

'Jealous?'

'No,' I say, offended. Even though it might be half true. 'Why would I be jealous?'

He whistles through his teeth. 'She's… well, she is a bit of a hottie.'

I roll my eyes.

'Actually, I'd never realised how much you two look alike until now.'

My heart stops for a second. That's a strange comment.

'But you've never met Tamara. How would you know?'

Lance shakes his head, completely nonplussed.

'That old graduation photo you have of you all, dummy. The one you keep in your bedside drawer.' His cheeks tint pink. 'Sorry. I was looking for something and came across it a few months ago.'

I say nothing but my skin crawls. My privacy has been invaded. And Lance thinks that my old friend is a hotter version of me. Great.

We watch Tamara drive through the water, the muddy surface left swirling in their wake, then we do the same.

'This is fun,' says Lance, putting his car into gear and gunning the engine as Tamara pulls away and disappears down the track.

Once we've crossed the water, we drive for about another twenty minutes until the forest and bushlands open to a clearing, where the holiday house – a gleaming white mansion – and the angry, churning Indian Ocean greet us like a slap to the face, waking us from our sleepy, long-journey-induced haze.

Once we've parked our cars, we get out and have a good stretch. It's a relief to inhale the fresh gusty air after being stuck in the car for so many hours.

Thankfully the rain has eased up a little, giving us time to get our luggage out of the car before the slate-grey clouds looming in the distance get to work on the storm the news has been banging on about for the last two days.

The large double wooden doors of the house fling open as we follow Tamara and the others up the veranda steps.

I hold my breath as I wait for my first glimpse of Lizzie.

Beautiful Lizzie, the most popular and gorgeous of the group. The blonde with all the curves in all the right places, and a witty, cheeky personality to match. All the guys used to go crazy for Lizzie.

But I gasp as she steps through the door.
Oh, Lizzie, I can't help but think.
What happened to you?

6

Lizzie had always been the head of our group. The girl born into wealth, who was also gifted by nature the most delicate bone structure I'm yet to find on the cover of a magazine, as well as the most unusual, lavender-coloured eyes. She's smart too, always got As back in high school, was voted class captain each year and was also the head of the school netball team.

Lizzie was officially invited to every party held during our teen years whereas the rest of us were usually the plus-ones, or plus-fours in our case. It was Lizzie, Angelica, Tamara, Sienna and me. Us five. If we were a band, Lizzie would be the mesmerising lead singer that nobody takes their eyes off. I'd probably be the drummer, hidden away at the back of the group.

When any of us started crushing on a guy, we felt compelled to tell Lizzie. She was always the first to know. When I look back now it seems utterly ridiculous to think that we used to run our crushes by Lizzie the leader, seeking her approval before we took things any further.

I guess that's the first thing that went wrong ten years ago. It was the first time I *didn't* tell Lizzie whom I had feelings for. Keeping my crush close to my chest was probably my biggest mistake. But he wasn't simply a crush. He was the love of my life. And most of all, my best friend. A one-in-a-million best friend.

'I can't believe you all came,' says this new, rail-thin, buzz-cut Lizzie, clasping her hands together and doing a little jump.

A sudden gust of salty wind blasts us as we all gather on the veranda, sending my hair flying around my face. Sienna squeals and we all laugh at her attempts at flattening her red hair. Lizzie laughs the hardest and loudest.

There's something off about Lizzie's excitement. Her smile is a little too eager, her laughter way too forced. She reminds me of the kids you see on the internet bawling their eyes out and then pasting on a huge smile for the camera because they are asked to do so by their parents who are likely the ones responsible for making them cry in the first place.

Lizzie is swept into Tamara's open arms, then, once Jake and Lucas step aside, Sienna swoops in for an extra-long hug. Lance turns and makes a sweeping motion with his hand for me to go first, so I force my legs to shuffle past him and set my bag down before mustering the courage to face Lizzie for the first time in ten years.

Lizzie's smile slips away as I approach her and when I wrap my arms around her body, I'm shocked at how rigid she feels against me. I don't know if it's because she is repulsed to be hugging me or if it's just the fact that she's so skinny now and doesn't have all those gentle curves padding her body anymore.

'Thanks for inviting me, Lizzie,' I say, giving her a quick squeeze.

She keeps her arms dangling by her sides, unlike when she hugged the others.

'I invited you both,' she says, moving her head past mine so that she can offer a bright, genuine smile to Lance. 'Are you going to introduce me to your man, Maz?'

All eyes are on me, and I can feel a flush of heat creeping up my neck and into my face. I clear my throat. 'Of course. Lizzie, this is Lance, my… m-my boyfriend.' I inwardly curse myself for allowing my nerves to get the better of me, while Lizzie watches me with a single raised brow. If I'm going to make it believable that I'm with Lance, I need to start saying it with more conviction.

Lizzie's lavender gaze falls on Lance, who stands there grinning at her. She grins back, then throws him a sexy little wink. 'Welcome to the holiday house, Lance.'

If you ignored the pale skin and the fact that her bones are showing through her clothes, I'd say the ghost of old Lizzie has been resurrected, revived by Lance, if the way she's beaming at him is anything to go by.

Jake and Lucas introduce themselves to Lizzie without so much as a quick nod from the hostess. Jake even extends a hand for Lizzie to shake, but she keeps her eyes firmly fixed on Lance the entire time, embarrassingly so. Everyone avoids my gaze. I can't blame them. This is an extremely awkward situation for them all. I wish I could say 'don't worry guys, we're not even together' but that would make things even weirder. Because then they'd know I lied to them about it and they'd start to wonder what's behind the lie.

'Come in,' Lizzie says, finally dragging her eyes away from Lance and stepping aside to allow us to enter the holiday house. 'Once you enter these doors, you sign up for a weekend of fun.'

'Yay,' says Sienna, as she hops onto Lucas's back and rides him like this through the open doorway.

Tamara turns and widens her eyes at me and I'm relieved to find that someone else has properly acknowledged how weird Lizzie is behaving towards Lance.

I grimace and Tamara giggles and I finally release the breath I'd been holding for way too long and find myself beginning to relax. I'd forgotten how nice it is to have someone understand you without having to speak a word. That's what I've missed the most about losing touch with my friends. That instinctive, almost psychic bond that develops between the people you experience all the trials and tribulations of growing up with.

With Lance and Jake in tow, Tamara and I carry our luggage inside together and follow Lizzie down the long hallway, the polished jarrah floorboards gleaming beneath the glittering chandelier suspended from the ceiling.

Yes, a chandelier at a beach house. But that's how Lizzie's mum, Sophie, rolls. She never does minimal. Never has. And this beach mansion, for all its opulence, shows a tiny bit of restraint compared to their riverside home in the city.

The other girls would get excited when invited to Lizzie's riverside home for sleepovers when we were in our early teens, because her house was so grand. But I secretly hated it. I always felt on edge whilst there, making sure not to touch anything or make a mess, or say anything stupid and uncultured in front of her parents. I could hardly wait for my mum to come pick me up and take me home in the morning so that I could finally relax and be myself.

But I'd always loved *this* place, the beach house. Yes, it's a bit fancy for the beach, but there's a more laidback energy here. How could it not be with the majestic Indian Ocean in its backyard, and a remote beach that stretches for miles on either side?

When we used to come here, one of the first things I'd do is go stand by the living room window or head up to the upstairs balcony and look out at the everlasting view of the sea, where I'd feel so connected to nature, so far removed from the chaos of life. It made me feel small and insignificant, which in turn made my problems disappear... only momentarily, of course.

Once Lizzie has shown the others their rooms, she leads Lance and I upstairs where there are only two bedrooms. Lizzie's favourite room, known as the white room, and her parent's bedroom, which nobody, not even Lizzie was ever allowed to use in the past.

Lizzie opens the bedroom door wide open, revealing a gorgeous white four-poster bed and snowy-white walls, the whiteness broken up by a peach-coloured throw draped across the bottom end of the bed and a few decorative peach cushions strewn across the head of the bed, just so.

'You two will be sleeping here.'

'In your favourite room?' I ask, surprised she didn't take it for herself. 'Where are you sleeping?'

Lizzie waggles her eyebrows and flashes a grin at Lance. 'Will and I will be sleeping in the master suite.'

'Will?'

'Yes, my partner. What, you don't think buzz-cut girls get the guys?'

'No, of course not... I didn't mean–'

'Relax, Maz.' Lizzie throws back her head and laughs, then winks at Lance again. 'Geez, when did she get so uptight, Lance?' She continues to laugh, rather psychotically if you ask me, until a large vein appears on her forehead, and she suddenly drops the laugh and looks me dead in the eye. 'Seriously, Maz, why would I invite everyone's partners if I didn't have one myself? I'm not into boyfriend stealing,' she says pointedly, and my breath catches in my throat.

Is she talking about what happened ten years ago? How would she know? And great. My hopes of us girls, now mature adults, settling our differences around a table loaded with good food and wine this weekend, is fading by the minute.

Lance puts a gentle hand to my lower back and clears his throat. 'Thanks, Lizzie.'

Lizzie's face transforms into something that can only be described as angelic.

'You are most welcome, Lance.'

Despite the muggy, humid air from the storm, a cold trickly feeling travels down my neck, and I have a strong desire to take my bags back downstairs and get the hell out of here.

Maybe Lizzie didn't invite us all here to put the past behind us, maybe she can't let things go. Maybe she wants answers. I mean, I want answers too. I think we all do. Because none of what happened that night makes sense.

But the way Lizzie's acting has me wanting to run away from this place and never look back. To hell with answers. To hell with cathartic healing. I'll just keep burying my trauma as deep as possible and get on with life as best I can.

'I'll leave you two to it,' she says, then she pauses in the doorway and smiles softly, her lavender eyes widening to the point of childlike innocence.

My stomach swirls with a wave of nausea. But when I look at Lance, he's gazing at Lizzie like he's mesmerised. 'Thanks again,' he says, smiling wide.

'No problem.' Lizzie's voice is soft and sweet as she steps away from the door to allow us to enter the room. 'While you're here with Marilyn, you're my extra special guest, Lance. What's mine is yours. Feel free to take what you like whenever you like.'

'Thanks, Lizzie,' I say, before shoving Lance into the room and shutting the door behind us.

Lance looks at me, a stupid grin on his lips. 'She's nice.'

'What the hell?' I whisper, pulling a face. 'I don't know why she's acting like this.'

Lance ignores me and crosses the room to stand by the huge ceiling-to-floor window which showcases the waves crashing against the shore and the black clouds rolling in.

'This place is unreal,' he says.

'Don't you think Lizzie is acting a bit flirty towards you?'

Lance finally looks at me and laughs. There's an arrogant twinkle in his eye and a swagger in his step as he closes the distance between us. He smirks at me and rests both hands on my waist. 'Aww, you're not jealous are you, Maz?' He waggles his brows. 'I tell you what, if you keep things interesting for me this weekend, I won't pay Lizzie any attention.'

I shove him in the chest and sit on the edge of the bed. It feels as soft as a cloud. Maybe I can sleep my way through this trip. Cocoon myself in this bed with its soft fluffy blankets, guzzle wine and watch the storm dance with the sea.

'No, I'm being serious. I think Lizzie has it in for me.' I stare out at the sea as the dark clouds open up, sending silvery sheets of rain down upon the water. It's a spectacular sight. But it also gets me worried. That's a hell of a lot of rain, and we already ran into trouble with that flooded dip in the track.

'What if we get stuck here? What if we decide to leave but we can't because of the flooding?'

I take my phone out of my pocket and groan.

'Oh I forgot this stupid place has no phone signal.' I get up. 'I'm going to go down and get the Wi-Fi code. At least this place has a landline.'

Lance's smug smirk softens into a genuine smile.

'Hey, wait a sec, come here first.' He draws me into a hug.

I inhale his familiar scent and drop my shoulders in efforts to relax.

'Everything is going to be fine, Maz. We're going to have a great time, and by the time we leave here the storm will have blown over and we'll easily drive out of this place.'

I rest my head against Lance's chest, finding comfort in the steady beat of his heart. But the sound is drowned out when the rain crosses over the sea and finally unleashes onto the house.

'I hope you're right,' I practically shout over the rain.

Lance chuckles and puts his lips to my ear.

'Oh, Maz, Lizzie is right about one thing. You do need to loosen up.'

Although I hate that he's agreeing with Lizzie, I sigh and drop my shoulders in defeat. 'I'll try.'

Lance gently rubs my back and shoulders. 'Maybe it'll help if you talk to me about what happened here ten years ago. Then I might be able to help you through this weekend.'

My heart palpitates at the suggestion. Although I came here with these exact intentions, now I'm not so sure I'm ready to share what happened with Lance, or with anyone here. Maybe I'll take my guilt to the grave.

'Can we just hug? I don't want to talk about any of that right now.'

'Okay, okay,' Lance says, soothingly, and continues to rub my back.

I snuggle into him and wrap my arms around his waist a little tighter, wondering how on earth I would cope if Lance wasn't here.

7

Then

The sun kisses my bare shoulders when I step out of the car, and I inhale deeply the fresh salty breeze, relishing the tang of it, the taste of the sea.

It was a hot and sweaty journey from the suburbs to Lizzie's holiday house on the south-west coast. Brayden's car's aircon decided to cark it halfway into the four-hour journey down here. But none of that matters now because we are here. An entire week at the most awesome beach house in the world with my best friends.

Last week I'd questioned whether we'd made the right decision in coming here instead of heading down to the official school leavers' celebrations in Dunsborough and Busselton with all the other graduates. But now that we're here – the vast Indian Ocean glittering beneath the sun, the cicadas making their music, a luxury house in the middle of nowhere all to ourselves – I know that we've made the right decision.

After Lizzie unlocks and opens the double front doors, we all pile inside, dragging our near-bursting luggage with us. I'd spent all week packing, carefully crafting a day outfit and night outfit for all seven days, even though deep down I know I'll end up wearing my favourite denim cut-offs and my tie-dyed T-shirt most of the time.

'Angelica and Samuel, cutest couple of the year, may have the rose room,' Lizzie says, putting on a haughty voice and indicating the door at the very end of the hallway with a flourish of her freshly manicured nails. The rose room is the biggest room at ground level and has the most gorgeous king-sized four-poster bed, with roses hand-carved into the wooden frame by a famous West Australian artist. I'm a little jealous, in more ways than one, but I get it. It's the 'romance' room so of course the only couple in the group is going to get it.

Lizzie grins at those of us still waiting with our bags, seeming to enjoy the fact that she's in charge of almost everything we do for this entire week. She's wearing her favourite colour, navy blue, which brings out her eyes – a pretty dress that stops at the very top of her toned thighs and leaves nothing to the imagination.

Brayden, Sienna's twin brother, wouldn't stop talking about Lizzie's 'thick' body the whole drive down. It got to a point where Sienna slapped him on the back of his head whenever he mentioned Lizzie. By the time we arrived at the holiday house she'd whacked him about twenty times, and he was complaining about a sore head.

Tamara, Sienna, Brayden and I stand in the hallway, relishing the musty-smelling but cool airconditioned breeze blowing against us that Lizzie turned on as soon as she walked through the door.

I'm secretly hoping that I'll get lucky and get to share Lizzie's upstairs room with her as it's got an ensuite. I'm funny about going to the toilet while others are within earshot, and everyone shares the downstairs toilet. But it would be even better if she let me and Tamara stay up there, because out of everyone in the group, Tamara is the one I'm closest to. But it is Lizzie's house, of course, and she's being generous enough already by letting us all celebrate our graduation here in the first place.

'Tamara and Marilyn, you two can have the blue room.' She grins at Brayden. 'Looks like you get a bedroom all to yourself, Bray.'

Sienna's face clouds over for a moment, but then confusion gives way to joy as a huge smile stretches across her face.

'So we're sharing the white room?' Sienna asks Lizzie, her voice whisper-quiet, as though unable to believe she's been bestowed such a gift.

Lizzie does a little dance. 'Of course, girl. I hope you don't like sleep. Because I don't plan on getting a wink this entire trip.'

Sienna's eyes twinkle. I'm not sure if she's tearing up with joy, but I guess she is one of the quieter ones of our group, and at times has claimed to be ignored by Lizzie, so I can understand why she's so excited. I'm happy for her.

But I'm even more happy for me and Tamara, as we get to share our room together, even though we don't get the luxury of an ensuite.

'Everyone, meet back here in bathers and boardies ready for a swim in ten minutes. I've got some sushi and vodka on ice. The party starts now, people,' Lizzie says, throwing her hands up in the air and swivelling her hips.

We all cheer and do our own little dances on the spot. I can't help but notice Lizzie sway a little bit closer to Brayden, who looks absolutely mesmerised by her hips and is no longer complaining about his sore head.

Lizzie is between boyfriends at the moment, and it looks as though Brayden is her bit of fun for the week. Poor guy has been crushing on Lizzie just about his whole life. And by the annoyed look on Sienna's face, I sense a potential meltdown in the near future, maybe after a bit of booze and sun. She didn't want her twin brother Brayden to come, but he and Lizzie are the only ones with their licence at the moment so Sienna begrudgingly allowed him.

Once we're in the blue room – a gorgeous room with sky-blue walls and clouds painted on them – Tamara and I dump our bags on the bed and join hands, doing our own private little dance, which is basically jumping up and down and screaming.

'This is going to be the best week ever!' Tamara says, flinging herself onto the queen bed made up with blindingly white linen. She rolls onto her back to stare up at the ceiling, which has tiny fairy lights strung across it, and sighs dramatically, putting a hand over her heart. 'I'm just so happy, Maz. Good things are coming to me, *finally*. I can feel it.'

I smile down at her but say nothing. I recognise that look, the misty eyes, the goofy grin, the flushed cheeks. Because I've seen it on my own face in the mirror a million times.

She's crushing hard. On someone she shouldn't crush on, because he's already taken.

I know this because I've got the same problem. Only I've had years of experience in hiding my feelings.

And that problem's name is Samuel.

Who also happens to be my best friend.

The same guy who right this minute is in the rose room with his girlfriend Angelica.

8

Now

I leave Lance and head downstairs to get the Wi-Fi code but as my foot leaves the last step, I collide against a tall, very firm body.

'Oh, I'm so sorry, are you okay?'

I look up and lock eyes with one of the most handsome men I've ever seen. He looks like he stepped right out of a British romcom and sounds like it too.

'I'm fine,' I say, my voice coming out high-pitched. I clear my throat and glance around for Lizzie or anyone else.

He smiles down at me, his dark eyes glittering with something I can't quite put my finger on, something that makes me think he might find me attractive. I'm not sure why he would. I don't exactly feel very attractive at the moment, not with my hair all over the place and an ex-boyfriend that reminds me, just by looking at him, that I wasn't enough during the course of our relationship.

'Will, honey.' Lizzie, who appears out of nowhere, is wearing a figure-hugging dress that reveals just how much weight she's lost over the past ten years.

My throat thickens with emotion. She has the body of an eight-year-old child. How did this happen?

'I see that Marilyn has wasted no time in getting to know you,' she says, smiling angelically despite the acid in her words.

Tamara, whose hair looks as though it's been through a tornado, appears at my side, sucking on her index finger, which looks to be bleeding. 'He bumped into her. It's not Marilyn's fault.'

Good old Tamara. I sneak a brief smile her way before turning my attentions back to Lizzie.

'We bumped into each other, no big deal.' I shrug, because this situation is beyond ridiculous. We're not in high school anymore. I don't need to explain my every movement to Lizzie. I'm a twenty-seven-year-old woman, for crying out loud.

Lizzie swallows and casts her eyes on the others who have started to gather around. 'Oh, I'm sorry. I didn't mean to make you feel like you have to explain yourself. It wasn't my intention at all.' She sighs and I catch an eyeroll as she glances away from me and focuses on Will. 'No one seems to understand sarcasm anymore so I guess I'll hold off for the rest of the weekend, just to be safe.'

I notice she has a large scar running along her scalp, a place where her short blonde hair doesn't grow.

Lance appears at the top of the stairs, frowning with confusion when he sees us all gathered below.

'What's going on?'

'Lance, honey.' Lizzie's voice is sickeningly sweet. 'Can I show you the bathroom upstairs in the master bedroom? There's something wrong with the shower and I'd like you to take a look at it.'

Lance shrugs and glances at me quickly before looking at Lizzie, palms out. 'I don't actually know a thing about plumbing.'

Lizzie climbs the stairs and when she reaches him, places a hand on his chest. I noticed when we arrived how bitten down her fingernails are. Who is this new Lizzie? Where are the shiny acrylics of old?

'Well, I'd still like you to take a look at it. Will's busy sorting something out for me, aren't you, baby?' She doesn't even take her eyes off Lance to look at Will as she tosses a set of keys down the stairs. They land at the base of the steps with a loud clank.

I pick them up and hand them to Will, feeling second-hand humiliation on his behalf.

Will blinks several times then takes them from me and nods up at Lizzie. 'Sure. I'll sort it right away.' He disappears out the front door.

I shake my head once Lance and Lizzie have gone upstairs, wondering what that was all about, the Lance and the Will part. Lizzie was never this odd back in the day. Sure, she liked to get what she wanted in life and lived to the beat of her own drum, but she was always honest in her dealings with everyone. She was never the type of girl to flirt with someone else's partner right in front of their eyes.

Tamara quirks an eyebrow at me. 'Um, that was weird.'

'I know. What's the deal with her obsession with Lance?'

'Who knows? But obsession is the correct word, that's for sure.' Tamara shakes her head and begins to smooth out her windswept hair. She tucks a thick lock of it behind her ears.

'You know, you look great,' I tell her because she really does. 'I honestly wouldn't have recognised you in the street.'

'Yeah. We've all changed,' she says, looking me up and down. 'But I think Lizzie has changed the most.'

I nod and gaze up at the top floor, trying to imagine what Lizzie is doing or saying to Lance right now. 'I'm worried about her. She doesn't look healthy. And she's not her happy, fun self. She seems… I don't want to say it because we're her guests and it's nice of her to invite us, but...'

'She's being an absolute bitch. You can say it.'

I gasp and put a hand to my mouth. 'Forget what I said a second ago, you haven't changed a bit, Tams,' I say, laughing. 'Always speaking facts.'

Tamara puts a palm against her ample chest and strikes a haughty pose.

'Hey, looks like you need a band-aid,' I say, noticing the fresh blood on her fingertip. 'Want me to get you one? I've got some in my bag.'

'Of course you do,' says Tamara with a laugh. 'Always the prepared one. I guess neither one of us has really changed.' She hides her hand behind her back. 'Nah, I'm good. It's just a tiny scratch. I was trying to pick some of those red wildflowers outside to decorate the table for dinner tonight but found out they're covered in prickles.'

Sienna appears out of nowhere and comes to stand beside us. 'Lucas has gone outside to find Jake and Will.'

'Oh, where did they go?' I ask.

Sienna shrugs. 'I don't know.'

'Lizzie wanted something looked at,' Tamara says. 'The generator in the basement, I think.'

'Oh,' I say, remembering the basement with a shiver. I'll never forget the way the hinges groaned when I opened the metal hatch that night ten years ago. I'll never forget that salty, metallic scent in the air. I'll never forget what I saw, the fear and horror that seized me when I slipped and lost my footing in the pool of warm blood. It's a place I've spent the past ten years trying my best to forget, which I've failed at, and I'm sure everyone here is the same. I'm surprised that Lizzie hasn't locked the basement up and thrown away the key.

Something thumps upstairs and it's followed by Lizzie giggling.

I tell myself not to worry. I'm not even dating Lance anymore so who cares? But I do. I can't help it. It feels like such a betrayal; not just from Lance, but Lizzie too.

Then again, I guess I deserve it. Maybe after ten years I'm finally getting my comeuppance.

I look at Tamara and Sienna. 'Hey, does anyone know the Wi-Fi password?'

As soon as the words leave my lips, the power goes out.

Thunder rumbles, much louder and closer than before, and lightning illuminates the floor-to-ceiling windows, casting flashes of light against our faces.

'Oh shit,' I say, when I realise what this means. 'There goes the Wi-Fi.' I stare down at my phone. 'No signal. No Wi-Fi. Awesome.'

'Oh my God. What if something happens? What if we need to call for help? With all this rain we could become trapped,' says Tamara.

Sienna takes a deep breath and puts a hand to her chest. Sienna used to have panic attacks all the time while we were in high school. I gently rub her back.

'Just breathe. It's going to be okay,' I say.

She nods and continues to take measured, calming breaths.

Tamara's eyes grow round with worry.

Lizzie and Lance finally come downstairs. Lance's face is flushed, and he looks uncomfortable and confused, his shirt ruffled at the collar.

But Lizzie's face bears no expression, she looks as cool and as pale as an ice queen.

'Looks like it's dinner by candlelight tonight,' says Lizzie, her lavender eyes dark round holes in the dimness of the room.

Thunder growls again and more lightning flashes, sending streaks of light zigzagging across Lizzie's face. I'm surprised to see that her eyes are filled with tears.

'Is everything okay?' Tamara asks, and Lizzie nods, not meeting any of our gazes.

The hairs on my neck stand on end. Something isn't right with Lizzie. The fact that Will went outside to take care of something for Lizzie and we lost power not long after is way too coincidental.

Lance comes to my side, slips his hand tightly around mine and says, 'Can we talk?'

9

'Here. Take a bottle of wine with you,' Lizzie offers from the kitchen. She reaches into the fridge and turns around, an icy bottle of sauvignon blanc in her hand. She opens one of the high cupboards and takes out two sparklingly clean wine glasses. 'Looks like you two might need a drink.'

What does she mean by this? Despite my reservations about this new version of Lizzie's motives, I take the offered wine and glasses and head upstairs with Lance. Lizzie is right about one thing, I'm going to need a drink and then some to get through this weekend.

Lance closes the bedroom door behind us. He flicks his head towards the window. 'That's some view.'

'It's stunning, isn't it? The most beautiful beach in the world.' I don't mention that it's also very difficult to look at because of the memories this piece of isolated coastline dredges up. But I don't shut the curtains, I force myself to gaze out upon the endless sand and the churning grey sea. The very place Samuel – the only guy I've ever truly loved – and I shared the most life-changing conversation of our lives.

'What happened here all those years ago, Maz?' Lance asks.

I quickly look away when he meets my gaze and when I don't respond to his question, he sighs and opens the wine then pours us each a glass.

'Thank you,' I say, noting the slight tremor in Lance's fingers as he passes the cold glass of white wine into my hand.

We don't tap our goblets like we usually do, which comes as a surprise because Lance is usually super merry with a drink in his hand. But Lance is not himself. Whatever occurred between him and Lizzie in the bathroom earlier has given him a furrowed brow and dark, pensive eyes.

I watch as he takes a sip of wine and gazes out at the sea, looking like a man with the weight of the world upon his shoulders.

'Are you okay?'

He turns to face me and a ghost of a smile visits his face before vanishing as quickly as it had arrived.

'Yeah. I'm just thinking about my family.'

I nod in understanding. I lost my dear mum last year and still find some days terribly difficult. The sadness can be unbearable at times. I can only imagine what it would feel like for Lance, to lose both his parents just like that. One minute they are alive and well, the next they are instantly killed in a car accident. At least with my mum, we had time to say our goodbyes to each other.

'You know you can talk to me about it anytime. I'm here for you, even though we're not together anymore.' I offer a supportive smile. 'I'm still your friend.'

He nods and takes another sip from his glass. I do the same and relish the tastes of the cool, citrusy wine against my tongue.

'I'm just starting to wonder if this was such a good idea,' he says. 'Maybe we should get our things and hop in the car and go find ourselves a nice hotel somewhere, just the two of us.'

This is odd. Lance was the one who encouraged me to go on this trip. And then when my car wouldn't start, he was more than eager to drive me here.

'Why the change of heart? Did something happen between you and Lizzie? Did she say something?'

Lance draws his head back and pulls a face, but he doesn't meet my eye.

I recognise that look. Great. So it took less than an hour for my 'fake' boyfriend to cheat on me, or at least think about cheating on me. I'm not even going to bother asking because what's the point?

I sit on the edge of the bed and the mattress sinks as Lance comes to sit beside me.

'What happened here, Maz? All those years ago. You never talk about it. But I can feel so much tension between you and your friends. Honestly, it's going to be a dud of a weekend if you guys don't sort out your differences.'

'Lizzie said something about me, didn't she?' My chest tightens in panic at the thought, even though I know that it's better that everyone knows, and that it's healthier for me to come clean and free myself from this secret once and for all. 'What exactly did she say?'

I always thought that nobody knew about me and Samuel and our conversation that night. As far as I know, we were the only two on that moonlit beach. Everyone else was playing strip poker inside the house. But if Lizzie does somehow know, then it would explain why she's been acting so weirdly around me. She must blame me for what happened.

Perhaps she's been holding on to this knowledge for the past ten years and that's why she is the way that she is today, so broken and so... strange. And although she has no right to blame me for what happened, I understand why she would, because I hold myself responsible for what happened. Maybe not directly, but my choices ultimately led to the most tragic event of our lives.

Lance stares out at the sea and drains his glass. He spins it around in his hands which are resting against his lap.

'Lizzie said nothing about you. But anyone can see that there's a weird vibe between you girls. Jake and Lucas have picked up on it too.'

'Since when are you buddies with Jake and Lucas?'

He shrugs.

'But yeah, I guess you're right. I was hoping this weekend would help us all to put the past behind us. That's why I think I should stay, that *we* should stay. Because I think this is probably my one opportunity to right my wrongs.'

Lance pours himself some more wine and tops up my glass.

'Did you do something wrong? Back then?'

'Please, Lance. Can we not discuss it now?' Why is he being so insistent about this? It's got to be Lizzie. She must have said something. One hundred percent. I wish she would let me deal with this myself, in my own way – even though I'm not sure how I plan to do that just yet.

'Look, if I'm going to try and enjoy myself here and be able to talk to my old friends about our past differences, I need to unwind first. Please.' I raise my glass and tap it against his, producing a musical chime. 'Let's just have a nice, quiet drink together, a little moment to ourselves. I need time to… think everything through.'

Lance sighs. 'Okay. But I still think that we'd be better off leaving right now and getting ourselves a hotel room.'

The idea of fleeing to a hotel room and never looking back, never seeing my old friends ever again, is so appealing I almost say yes. But I don't because I know I can't run anymore. I need to stay and deal with this, once and for all.

'I'm sure by the time we leave here on Sunday we'll both be thankful that we came.'

Lance takes a large gulp of wine, his eyes dark. 'Okay. I hope you're right.'

I shiver and take another sip, the alcohol spreading through my veins and offering some inner warmth. It's not like Lance to be so pessimistic.

I glance around the room, at the high ceilings, then at the choppy sea. The hairs on the back of my neck prickle. What is it about this place that changes us all? That makes us do things we normally wouldn't back home in our everyday lives.

We sit together, not speaking, while we watch the Indian Ocean get lashed by the rain as lightning cuts across the angry, bruised sky. It is all at once brutal yet strangely calming.

But our moment of stillness is soon broken by the front door slamming shut and a shout coming from downstairs, followed by a thin scream that turns my blood cold.

'Did you hear that?' I put a hand to my thudding heart and set my wine glass down on the bedside table. 'I wonder what's happening?'

Lance gives me a dark look.

'Can we even trust these people? You haven't spoken to them in over ten years, Maz.'

I say nothing.

Because I'm sure he wouldn't like my answer.

10

Then

Sam has been my best friend since kindergarten. He is also the guy I am secretly in love with. I won't ever admit to it though, because I know that Samuel has only ever seen me as a friend, or worse, a sister, so I know that nothing will ever happen between us in the romantic sense. Also, his girlfriend Angelica is my friend, so I would never try to come between them or attempt to make her feel uncomfortable around me.

To be honest, I've learned to simply love Sam from afar and be grateful that we're besties, that he's still a huge part of my life.

'What do you think?'

I blink and my awareness returns to the blue room – the bedroom Tamara and I are sharing for the week.

Tamara is posing, hands on hips, showing off her white bikini that really sets off the tan she was lucky enough to get from a family trip to Bali in October. She's so tall and slim with a perfectly narrow waist and legs for miles.

'Does it make me look too flat-chested?'

'Seriously? You look amazing. You've got the body of a model.'

A model's body I'd die to have. But it's not to be. I've been blessed with the family trait all women on my mum's side of the family have inherited for generations.

Big boobs. Not just big. Enormous ones. Two of my aunts had reduction surgery. If it wasn't for the expense, I'd do the same. It's a pain in the arse not being able to find clothes that fit and there's nothing worse than the creeps at pubs and clubs, or even walking down the street, staring at my chest drooling as though someone has performed an on-the-spot lobotomy on them.

'Oh shush. You're the model here,' Tamara says, but her eyes are on her reflection in the mirror as she adjusts her bikini top in a bid to make her boobs appear more fleshed out.

I feel pasty and a bit blah in my black full-piece suit that I had to buy from the granny range at the shops because the teenage bathers would get me arrested for indecent exposure, but Tamara assures me that I look like a 'vampy hottie' with my long black hair and pale skin, so I walk out of the bedroom wearing my bathers and my cut-off denims feeling somewhat confident.

That is, until we walk into the living room, and I see all the girls looking amazing in their bikinis. Samuel gives me a gentle smile and a thumbs up when he sees me. He knows about my insecurities and always does his best to cheer me up. Maybe I fell in love with him because he's the one guy who's never made a big deal out of my chest.

But something's wrong. Even though he has his arm around Angelica, I can tell by the frown on his face and the way he keeps scratching the back of his neck that something is bothering him. They've been having problems of late. Lizzie told me privately, last week at school, that she thinks the couple will split before the end of our leavers' week.

I just know that Samuel is going to be a wreck if that happens, because he loves her so much – at least I think he does. Sam's dated a lot of girls, but Angelica is someone he's fallen head over heels for in a way I've never seen him do. He talks about her all the time, his face lights up whenever he sees her. It's sweet, and yes, I'm jealous. But Angela is such a kind, good friend, and if I had to choose anyone for Sam to be with then it'd be her.

'Boys, you carry the esky between you,' says Lizzie. She puts an arm each around Tamara and my neck and draws us close to her side. The smell of the coconut-and-lime-scented body spray Lizzie uses tickles my nostrils. 'Let's hit the beach, guys.'

We spill out of the house, singing and dancing to the music booming out of Brayden's speaker, towels over our shoulders and a bottle of sunscreen being tossed between us.

The November sun is merciless in the cloudless sky, and once we've settled on a spot right in front of the water, I make sure to add an extra layer of sunscreen once my first lot has sunk in. I've got to be extra careful not to get too burnt on my first day or I'll be spending the rest of the trip inside. And there's no way I'm going to miss out on all the fun.

'Honestly, Maz, you may as well come to the beach in a wetsuit if you're going to wear that much sunscreen,' says Samuel, grinning at me.

I'd playfully kick some of the pristine white sand at him if it wasn't going to stick all over my sunscreen-covered legs, so instead I continue rubbing the pineapple-and-coconut-scented cream into my body, feeling happy that Samuel decided to come on this trip.

Lizzie had messaged me yesterday saying she was worried Angelica and Samuel were going to cancel on us at the last minute. But thank God they decided to come.

I always feel safe with Samuel around. He's always felt like family, like the other half of me. We understand each other in a way the others never will. Sam and I are the only two of the group who attended our elite private secondary school for free on scholarships, whereas the others' parents had to pay a lot of money for their kids to attend such a prestigious school.

Once I'm completely smothered in cream and smelling like a piña colada, I spread out my towel and sit on it cross-legged. The rest have already arranged themselves in a circle around the esky, which sits at the centre like a deity we're all worshipping.

Lizzie ceremoniously pops the white lid off. The ice makes a crunching sound as she digs around with her hand, and she woops when she finds what she's looking for.

'I present to you, our reward for putting up with school for twelve long and torturous years of our lives.'

The sparkly label on the one-litre bottle of vodka glistens in the sun as chunks of ice drip down the glass.

We all cheer and clap as Lizzie breaks the seal and screws off the cap.

'To us! No more sitting in boring-ass classrooms anymore. No more having to listen to Principal Prickface drone on about discipline and integrity every week at assembly.'

'Hear, hear,' I say, and we all clap and cheer when she takes the first swig of the bottle.

She passes it to me, the icy bottle cool against my palm. I think carefully before I raise it to my lips.

'No more Mr Hanson checking my skirt length with a ruler,' I say, before taking a huge glug from the bottle. Laughter fills the air and I giggle and relish the cool burn as the alcohol slides down my throat.

'Eww he's such a creep,' says Sienna, accepting the bottle from me. It almost slips from her tiny hands. She thinks for a minute, her hair falling over her brown eyes. 'I'll miss Mr Lannin, because he's cool, so, let's drink to Lannin.'

'To Lannin,' we all chorus, as Sienna raises the bottle and tips her head back.

'Yum,' she says, grimacing as she breaks out in a full-body shiver and heaves the bottle over to Samuel who gladly receives it.

'No more old Mrs H asking me about my "home life",' he says, meeting my gaze and raising his brows before gulping down way too much and choking and spluttering vodka all over Angelica's bare arm.

Angelica sighs with frustration and glares at her wet arm. 'I'm going swimming to get this off.'

'I'll come too,' says Samuel, blinking, his eyes still watering from the coughing fit.

'No,' Angelica says coldly. 'I want to swim *alone*.'

Sam says nothing and stares down at the sand. I catch Tamara watching him closely for a few seconds and then I see her glare at Angelica as she dives into the glittery ocean.

Sweat beads down my back. The heat of the sun on my skin is unbearable. I'd go for a swim right now if Angelica wasn't so insistent on going alone. But I want to respect her need for personal space, so I'll wait another ten minutes before I go for a little dip. If she's still swimming then I'll go over to her and ask if she needs someone to talk to. If she doesn't, then that's fine. The Indian Ocean is the third largest ocean in the world, so there's plenty enough space for us all.

Sam catches my eye and releases a heavy sigh. I make a face, one that I hope expresses my sympathy for his troubles. He mouths at me, 'talk later' and I nod.

Brayden has the vodka now and shrugs then shouts, 'Fuck school!' before he takes a big swig from the bottle.

Everyone cheers in agreement.

Tamara takes the bottle next, and I can't help but notice that her blue eyes are red and shiny, when they weren't a moment ago.

'I'm going to miss this. Us,' she says, nodding at us all in a sad way before taking a sip.

Her toast casts a slight melancholic tone over our moods. Even Brayden looks pensive.

'We need food,' Lizzie says abruptly.

She takes out a plastic tray filled with rows of the most delicious-looking sliced nori rolls and sets it on top of the esky lid. 'Go for it, guys. This is our stomach lining. I've got an entire fridge loaded with drinks; enough for the whole week so, get eating.'

'Yum!' Sienna says, taking two of the brown rice and tuna rolls and a small fish-shaped soy sauce. 'Thanks.'

We all help ourselves, except for Sam who has gone after Angelica.

I lean forward and take a couple of California rolls, sneaking a peak at Sam and Angelica in the water. It's not looking good for Samuel, who's raking his hands through his long dark fringe, which is something he does whenever he's anxious. And by the rigidness of his body, I can tell he's stressed out.

Sam says something, but he's got his back to us, so I can't hear it over the shrieking gulls that are now hovering over our sushi.

But we hear Angelica, who is facing us, swear in frustration, which is unlike her. Then she shouts, 'You had no right to read that letter, it's personal. Now go away!'

Samuel hangs his head and wades out of the water and back to shore.

I sit back down and shove a California roll in my mouth, almost choking on it when I catch Lizzie watching me with a narrowed gaze.

'Let's play truth or dare tonight,' she says, grinning wickedly, mischief lighting up her lavender eyes.

The others cheer.

But I don't.

11

Now

Lance doesn't let me go first, so I follow him close behind, clutching at his shirt as we descend the staircase slowly, pausing and straining to listen at each step. Outside the rain continues to fall, only softer now. It'd be cosy if it were any other house, but out here in the middle of nowhere, it just makes me feel claustrophobic.

About halfway down the stairs, Lance's tense muscles relax beneath his shirt then he turns to me and half-smiles. 'It's okay, nobody died. Well, at least, I don't think anyone did.'

I release my sweaty grip on Lance's shirt, leaving crease marks behind. If only he knew the significance of his words.

When we reach the base of the stairs, I can see that everyone has gathered in the kitchen. Sienna has her head in her hands and Lizzie is rubbing her back.

'What happened?' I ask, coming to stand beside Tamara.

'The generator is broken, so no power. Sienna's a little... upset by it, that's all,' she says, giving me a knowing look.

I relax a little, but not too much. Sienna used to have panic attacks about tests back in high school. So this is nothing new. But I do empathise with Sienna on this one. Having no access to the outside world isn't going to help me sleep tonight.

'Will thinks someone tampered with it,' says Lucas, eyeing us all with suspicion.

'Great,' I say, more unease creeping up my spine.

'Who would do that?' Sienna asks, a hysterical edge to her voice. 'Maybe it just broke because it's old.'

'Just breathe,' says Lizzie soothingly as she continues to rub circles on Sienna's back.

Lucas hovers nearby, frowning at Lizzie and looking like he wants to tell her to back off. He might be one of those over-protective boyfriends.

'Maybe we should think about leaving,' he says, glancing up at us all. 'With the storm coming...' Lucas shakes his head. 'The weather's bad enough already and now we have no power, no way of calling for help.'

'Why would we need help?' Lizzie asks, frowning then widening her eyes over Sienna's head at Lucas. 'We're safe here. The storm can't hurt us.'

Lucas doesn't respond, but I'm certain everyone in the room agrees with his concerns. I know I do.

Thunder growls scarily close, followed seconds later by flashes of lightning which illuminate the dim house momentarily.

'There we go, we've got all the light we need,' says Jake, grinning, his single blue eye darting between us all.

Nobody laughs.

I glance at Lance, who, by the delighted look on his face, is excited by the lack of electricity. It seems the anxiety he felt up in the room only minutes ago has miraculously vanished. Either that, or he's just putting on a front and wanting to act tough in front of the other men.

'Come on, people,' he says. 'We can still have a fun weekend. It'll be like camping. Except, a mansion instead of a tent. You know, like glamping. Kind of.'

Almost everyone looks at Lance like he's grown an extra head. Jake makes a noise in his throat and looks away. I get the strange feeling he doesn't like Lance for some reason. It makes me feel protective of my ex-boyfriend. I shift a little closer to his side.

Only Lizzie nods in agreement. 'We've got candles. But I'll send Will out to get more from town. Just in case.'

'In case what?' Sienna asks between controlled breaths, her eyes wide.

Lizzie doesn't respond.

'Where is Will?' Tamara asks, frowning. I can tell she doesn't think much of Lizzie's boyfriend already. But Tamara has always been like that, suspicious of newcomers.

Right on cue, Will bursts into the house, his dark curly hair pasted against his forehead and his wet white T-shirt clinging to his sculped muscles. He looks like he's come here straight from a Calvin Klein photoshoot, a very wet one.

Lance lightly elbows me in the ribs and mutters, 'Close your mouth, bub.'

I roll my eyes at him. Only Lance would joke at a time like this.

'Perfect timing, Will,' says Lizzie. 'I need you to duck out and get some extra candles.' She grins. 'But you might need to get changed first, hon.'

Will shakes his head, no laughter in his dark eyes. 'I won't be going anywhere. None of us will. The track is completely flooded. We're trapped.'

12

Sienna's dark eyes film over with tears. 'Oh my God. It's happening. I knew it. I knew they wouldn't rest. They're going to come for us. Get their revenge. She was right.'

'Sienna,' says Lucas, pinching his brow, unable to hide his frustration, 'nobody is coming for us. Come on. We've discussed this.' He lowers his voice but we can all still hear him. 'That woman was a charlatan out for your money.'

'Who and what are you talking about?' asks Jake, his single eye wide as he regards Lucas and Sienna with interest. 'Is there something we should know about this place?' he asks nobody in particular. He glances at all of us but then his single-eyed gaze rests on me.

I look away, my heart pounding rapidly. Of course, it's just by chance that Jake looked at me. Surely. Finally he looks away without saying anything. Hmm. Maybe he does know about what happened here ten years ago. Maybe everyone knows. The girls could have lived these ten years secretly holding me responsible.

Accusations were certainly thrown around between us at the time. The police couldn't solve the case. They wouldn't share any details with us during questioning, but we all knew that they had suspicions that one or more of us was involved. But ultimately, they didn't have enough proof and the case has remained unsolved.

Sienna continues to stare ahead, her dark lashes wet with tears, as though watching apparitions dance before her. She blinks rapidly and backs away as though genuinely terrified.

Lizzie abandons Sienna, her upper lip curled in disgust, and in an instant Lucas softens, his earlier irritation gone as he swoops in where Lizzie left off. He slips an arm around Sienna's waist, gently guiding her into the living room where he sits her down on the soft, cream leather couch and settles in beside her.

My heart softens to see how devoted Lucas is to my old friend. It's very clear to see that Sienna has found one of the rare good ones, and I'm happy for her.

'Can I get you anything?' I ask Sienna, as I crouch by her side.

She looks at me and shakes her head, her face ashen. She is genuinely spooked.

'I'm scared, Maz. After last time… we shouldn't have come.'

My heart races at the ominous tone in Sienna's words and the meaning behind them. She's right. We should never have come. And to think that I imagined, when first invited, that we'd be sitting around a table giggling away as we reminisced about old times. Somehow, I don't think that's going to happen now. Nor the lying on the beach beneath an umbrella reading a good book. Definitely not with this freak November storm. I rub my arms, wishing I'd packed more wintery clothes despite us being only days away from summer.

I'm not sure any amount of warm clothes would be able to shake this shivery feeling though, not until we drive out of this place tomorrow. That is, if it's at all possible to do so after all this rain.

'It'll be okay,' I say, stroking a short lock of cherry-red hair from her forehead. 'Once we've got the candles lit, it'll be cosy. We'll unpack some food, and all of us can have a nice catch-up.' I glance over my shoulder at the seemingly permanent veil of rain hanging over the grey sea. 'It can't rain forever. I'm sure this storm will pass overnight. It won't take long for the track to dry up.'

Sienna closes her eyes. 'I hope you're right.' She smiles and shakes her head. 'You've always been right. Little Miss Nerd. I remember feeling so proud when you won the dux award in year twelve.'

I smile, glad to see Sienna smiling and looking more relaxed. Finally, we're reminiscing about old times. Good times.

'Yeah, but what's the use of all those As when all you do is work as a waitress all day long?'

I turn around and see Lizzie standing there smirking at me.

'That's a horrible thing to say, Lizzie,' says Tamara, who comes to stand beside Lizzie, hands on hips.

'Tamara and Lizzie arguing,' says Sienna, forcing a chuckle in attempts to lighten the mood. 'This takes me right back.'

'How did you know I'm a waitress?' I ask Lizzie. 'We haven't spoken in over ten years.'

Lizzie shrugs and looks away. 'I don't know. Someone told me.' She shrugs again. 'Who cares? I think we all need a drink. Come on, girls, come help me unpack all the food and booze.'

Sienna rolls her eyes at me and surprises everyone when she gets up and follows Lizzie into the kitchen. Tamara and I lock eyes, and after I shrug my shoulders we both sigh dramatically and follow the other two, Jake trailing behind us. In a weird way it's nice stepping back into our old roles, and if anything it helps me to shake the eerie feeling that Lizzie... or someone... is up to no good.

While I'm packing expensive-looking parcels of cold meats and cheeses into the fridge, Lance appears and leans casually against the kitchen counter.

'Will wants his phone,' he says to Lizzie, while tapping his fingertips against the marble benchtop.

Lizzie, who had been singing joyfully while tipping a bag of organic corn chips into a large white bowl, scowls at him.

'Why? The track's flooded so it's not like he can go anywhere with it.'

Lance shrugs. 'We're all going to split up and walk around with our phones and check for signal.'

'In the middle of a storm? You're all crazy. Will does not need his phone,' Lizzie says.

I don't know why Lizzie is being so weird about Will wanting his phone. I'm happy that someone is being proactive. When he comes back, I'll be the first one asking him where to go for the phone signal if he's successful in finding it.

'So which is it?' Lance asks, ignoring Lizzie's whining.

She stares at all three phones charging on the bench.

'I... I don't know,' she says, her face turning pink beneath her delicate, translucent skin.

'How do you not know your own boyfriend's phone?' Tamara asks.

Lizzie gives Tamara daggers. 'He changes his phones like his underwear so I'm sorry if I don't keep tabs on what his latest iPhone looks like.'

Tamara turns and shoots me a wide-eyed, raised-brow look. I keep my face blank because Lizzie is staring right at me now.

Will comes in and without a word grabs the blue phone in the middle. He flicks a glance at Lizzie, and something passes between them as their eyes lock.

Tension fills the room, so much so that Jake, who hasn't said a word since we entered the kitchen, backs away from us all, grimacing, then turns and walks down the hallway. A few seconds later, he opens the front door, inviting the howling wind into the house before the door slams shut behind him.

Will pockets his phone, lightly shrugs his shoulders at Lizzie, and without a word, turns and follows Jake.

13

Then

My stomach stops churning after I've thrown up the contents of it over a patch of seagrass. But my head is still plagued by a chronic pounding against my skull. That vodka, combined with the heat of the sun, has got me drunker than I'd planned on getting. And by the looks of things, everyone else is suffering from the same problem.

Sienna is flat on her back, passed out along the shore, and Brayden, unsteady on his feet, is attempting to drag his sister away from the foaming water. After a few attempts, he manages just that and flops down beside her further up the beach where the sand is soft and white.

I dig around beneath the jumble of our beach towels, and half-empty packets of potato chips, searching for my phone, but can't find it anywhere. Although there's no signal out here on the beach, on this entire property to be exact, I'd like to at least know the time.

Sweat trickles from the base of my neck down my back. The skin on my shoulders sizzles. I can't remember the last time I applied sunscreen... did I put on another layer? Has it been hours? My face feels hot too. Oh God. I'm going to pay for this tomorrow. My mum is going to kill me if I come home covered in blisters and peeling skin.

Someone groans from behind and I turn to find Lizzie on all fours, crawling towards me, strands of her long blonde hair stuck to her face where she's been sick.

'Not you too,' I say. 'We're a bunch of lightweights, aren't we?'

Lizzie sits up and wipes the hairs from her face. 'It's this bloody sun,' she says, as though it's an uninvited guest who showed up unexpectedly on this trip. 'And… maybe the sushi went bad… on the way down here. I don't think I can look at another tuna roll without chucking ever again.'

'Same.' I open the esky and scoop out a handful of ice. 'But I bet we'll all be drinking again within twenty-four hours.' I grin, but it hurts my face. I press some of the ice to my face and pray my sunburn doesn't blister up tomorrow. 'Here.' I offer a handful of ice to Lizzie. 'This'll make you feel better.'

Lizzie takes the ice and begins rubbing it all over her face and chest. 'Oh yeah, this is the stuff.'

I do the same again with a fresh handful and sigh with relief. It feels so good. Once the ice melts I take another lot and proceed to rub the cubes over my body, groaning as the cool ice soothes my sunburnt shoulders.

'So what do ya think's up with Samuel and Angelica? Has he said anything to you about it?' Lizzie asks casually. But I know that her question is for Angelica's benefit, and she'll likely relay every word I say to her.

The ice has melted now, and I feel a little cooler and clearer-headed. I close the esky and enjoy the way the faint sea breeze feels cool against my wet skin.

'He hasn't. But I know that he cares about her. A lot,' I say, thinking about Sam's promise to talk later. Maybe he'll open up about what's wrong.

'Sam gets pretty full on quickly, doesn't he?'

'What do you mean?' I straighten my back. Although I hate showing it, I can't help but feel extra protective of Samuel whenever someone criticizes him. It's an automatic reflex, but sometimes I worry it'll make my feelings for him obvious. I'm normally pretty good at hiding it, but the vodka has weakened my vigilance.

'I mean, he just seems so... emotionally invested when he's in a relationship.' Lizzie shrugs. 'I don't know any teenage boys like that. And I've dated a lot. It's like... I don't know, as if he was ready for marriage after a week of dating Ange. I don't know. He's a bit... needy.' Lizzie shudders. 'I don't know how she puts up with him.'

'Is she not happy with him? Has she said something about breaking up with him?' I cringe at the eagerness and excitement in my voice.

Lizzie looks at me. 'No. Why? Has he said something about breaking up with her?'

'No,' I say, my voice flat now. 'Not at all.'

'Then what's bothering them?'

I shrug, thinking about what Angelica shouted at Sam when she was in the water.

'What's all this about a letter?' I ask. 'What letter did Sam read?'

Lizzie's eyes skip away. 'That's private. Who Angelica writes to is her own business.'

'Is it a guy?'

Lizzie shrugs. 'Maybe. So what? The girl can't have a pen pal?'

I don't have anything to say to that, because of course she can have a pen pal. But who in this day and age writes letters when we've got our phones and can instantly message our thoughts across? This guy must be pretty special for her to take the time to put pen to paper for him.

'You want them to break up, don't you?' Lizzie says, narrowing her gaze.

'What? No way. I think they're great together.' My traitorous face heats up, but hopefully she'll assume it's sunburn making my face red.

'You want Samuel for yourself, don't you?' Lizzie gets up, then falls over, then gets up again. She wobbles as she stands over me, shaking a finger.

Gulls soar across the sky above her and I have to shield my eyes from the bright glare of the sun with my hands.

'Stay away from Angelica and her boyfriend... he's not your property. And I'll be keeping my eyes on you this whole week... so watch yourself.'

'Sit down, Lizzie. You're being... ridiculous... and you're drunk.'

'And you're not?'

'We're all drunk. Maybe we shouldn't be having these kinds of conversations until we're sober.'

Lizzie shrugs. 'Yeah... okay, maybe you're right. Sorry, Maz. I'm a bitch when I'm drunk.'

I watch as Lizzie stumbles her way towards the sea before diving in. For a few seconds, when I don't see her head break the surface, my heart races in panic, but then her blonde head pops up several metres away and she starts doing backstroke, her face angled up at the afternoon sun.

Someone stumbles towards me from the distance, and after I blink away the blind spots, I see that it's Samuel. He collapses onto the mess of towels.

'Ouch,' he says, and rolls onto his side to reveal my phone poking against his bare hip bone where his board shorts have slid down.

'There it is.' I brush the sand off and shield the screen with my hand so that I can read the time. 'Shit. It's 4pm. We've been out here for hours. My mum will kill me when sees me burnt to a crisp. I hope I don't get blisters.'

'Can she kill me too? Because right now I want to die.'

I start to laugh but then stop when I see the look of pain etched across Samuel's features.

'Why do you want to die?'

Sam reaches for a packet of chips and I quickly snatch it out of his hands when I see which ones they are. 'Wait. These could have nuts in them.' I wave the bag in his face. 'See, satay chicken flavour. Let me read the ingredients.'

'Good. I'll eat them and die. Death by chips.'

'Don't you dare talk like that, or even joke about it.'

I squint my eyes at the tiny writing on the packet and gasp when I see nuts listed. 'Who on earth brought these with them? From now on, you're checking with me before you eat anything, understood?' I throw the packet as far away as possible and turn back to Samuel. 'I could never live without you... and I don't even want to imagine what that would be like.'

He looks at me, his blue eyes bloodshot, his forehead and cheeks red from the sun. 'Really?'

'Of course. You're my best friend. You mean the world to me.'

More than you'll ever know.

Samuel rolls onto his back and closes his eyes, a soft smile on his face. My lower belly flutters as my eyes do a quick sweep over Sam's half-naked body, and oh God, those damn kissable lips. Angelica is so lucky I could cry.

'That's so nice to know. And for the record, I don't want to die... not yet anyway.' He sighs. 'I just don't want to feel this way.'

'What way?' I shuffle closer to him and graze his fingers with my own.

A flock of gulls fly over us, their grey wings golden in the light of the afternoon sun.

Samuel's sandy fingers close around mine.

'I don't know, Maz. Confused. Lost. Just not myself.'

14

Now

Thunder rumbles again, rattling not only my bones but my nerves. The wind picks up, hammering the rain against the house. The windows and roof groan against the pressure and the girls and I jump when we hear a loud crack, followed immediately by a thump outside.

'What on earth was that?' Sienna asks, a packet of salted crackers in her hands. 'See, I told you all something bad was going to happen. I should have listened to my psychic.'

'You have a psychic?' Tamara asks, raising her brows.

She sneaks a glance at me and widens her gaze, but I ignore her. Poor Sienna is clearly anxious right now. We need to calm her down, not judge her.

'I'm going to go see if the guys are okay,' I say, setting down the chilled bottle of bubbly I uncorked a few seconds ago. 'I'd say that crack was a tree branch snapping in the wind.' I make a point to smile at Sienna. 'This house was built by Lizzie's dad, so it's built not only beautifully, but tough too. He was the best of the best. We'll be safe.'

Lizzie looks at me and holds my gaze, her eyes filming over with emotion. I remember reading about her dad passing in an online news article last year. He was a well-known luxury home designer lauded by many as one of the best in the country. He was also a genuinely nice guy and a good dad to Lizzie.

'You knew,' she says, blinking away the shine of her unshed tears.

'Yeah. Sorry I didn't reach out. We'd all been out of touch for so long... it didn't feel right.' It doesn't feel good now either. It feels worse. What kind of friend doesn't offer condolences to someone who has lost their dad?

Lizzie's face softens and she surprises me by reaching out and giving my hand a squeeze. Her fingers are warm against my cold ones.

'It's okay.' She lightly shrugs, but not in an offensive way. 'I knew your mum died and didn't reach out to you either. So I'd say we're even. I'm terrible when someone dies. I never know what to say and usually say the wrong thing.'

I sigh and we share a smile. 'Same here.' I feel like Lizzie and I have finally connected on something.

Sienna smiles and opens her arms. 'Aww, how about a group hug?'

Tamara raises her brows and takes a step away from Sienna. 'Um, I'm going to go get changed. You guys can enjoy your creepy hippy hug without me.'

Sienna watches as Tamara disappears down the hallway towards the bedrooms, and frowns. 'I think she's upset about something. I might go talk to her.' She puts an arm around each of us and squeezes us towards her tiny birdlike body. 'I'm feeling better already, guys. Thank you.'

'No worries,' I say. 'That's what friends are for.'

Sienna's perfume tickles my nose. I'm sure I've smelt this particular floral scent before. I'm about to ask her what kind she's wearing when a roll of thunder cracks so loudly we all jump. A streak of lightening follows, illuminating the darkening sky through the kitchen window.

Sienna yelps and abandons us to scurry after Tamara.

Lizzie and I share a grin.

'Hey,' she says, 'do you want to brave the elements with me and go search the basement for extra candles?'

All the warm and fuzzy feelings from our recent touching moment are replaced by an icy sensation that snakes through my veins and leaves me stone cold.

How can Lizzie just casually mention the basement like that, when it's the very place it all happened?

'Really? Now?'

She shrugs and frowns at my reaction. 'Sure. Why wouldn't we? We need candles, dork. I doubt the power is going to magically come back on through the night.'

I tell myself to relax. That Lizzie is right and that I am being ridiculous. This is her second home and she used to come here with her family all the time and likely still did after what happened. She's had more good memories here than bad, even if the bad one is a horrific one. Plus, she's likely had to venture down to the basement a number of times over the past ten years.

Lizzie heads towards the front door and turns back to face me when her hand is on the brass doorknob.

'So are you coming or not, Maz?' she asks, as the wind whistles through the cracks in the door. She raises her brows. 'Or does the idea of going down into the basement bring back too many painful memories for you?'

She turns her head and mutters something in a lowered voice, something that I don't quite catch.

Tiny wings of fear flutter inside my stomach, but I ignore my instincts and follow Lizzie anyway. I'm not sure if I'm just being stubborn or if I'm trying to prove a point.

Either way, I'll have to face the basement whether I'm ready or not.

15

'Of course it brings back painful memories.' I don't hide the irritation from my voice. 'I think about them all the time, and to be honest, going down there scares the crap out of me.'

Lizzie's face softens again. That's twice in the space of a few minutes. It's like she's battling this need to hate me even though she knows deep down that we've both suffered equally at the hands of loss.

'For the record, I think about them every day too,' she says, as I come to stand by the door at her side. 'I dream about them as well. All the time.' She rolls her eyes and smiles. 'And it took me ages to get over my fear of the basement. The first year was hard. I had to go down with my mum, holding her hand the entire time.' Lizzie shrugs. 'But now it just feels like any other room in the house.'

She turns and opens the door before I get the chance to respond and the sheer force of the wind takes my breath away as it pushes against us and blows everything off the coat rack by the door, sending umbrellas, hats and coats sliding across the hallway's polished floor.

'Quick!' Lizzie grabs my hand and we both brave the elements, pulling the door shut behind us and running for the basement trapdoor down the left-hand side of the property, our hair whipping around our faces.

When we reach the trapdoor, Lizzie unhooks the padlock and tosses it aside. The wind flips the metal hatch open, slamming it against the concrete floor.

'Get in,' Lizzie shouts over the howling wind and rain.

I have no time to worry over my fears and my skin-prickling reservations about facing the very place that still gives me nightmares to this day. But maybe this is the best way, to just face it head on.

Despite the wobble in my legs, it ends up being somewhat of a relief to begin the descent down the stone staircase and escape the brutality of the weather. The cool, musty air of the basement feels practically cosy after being whipped around by the storm. Once my feet hit the grey cement floor of the basement, I experience a wave of nausea.

In order to calm my racing heart, I take a deep breath and then another while Lizzie follows behind me, looking pale.

It's like stepping back through time, I think, as I glance around. The daylight, although gloomy, is enough to allow me to see once my eyes adjust. The basement, although missing the little wooden table that I found my best friend slumped against, is almost exactly the same as it was ten years ago.

I wonder if Lizzie's parents had come down to remove the table and chairs before Lizzie came back here for the first time after it all happened. They probably hired cleaners to scrub the bloodied last step and the floor at the base of the stairs. I'm too scared to look too closely in case I see any tell-tale rust-coloured stain.

'So, where are the candles?' I ask, my words coming out strained and high-pitched as I shiver beneath my damp clothes.

Lizzie wipes her damp face with her shirt and glances towards a dark area which escapes the light coming down from the trapdoor, where two wooden credenzas sit side by side.

'Should be in that first cupboard. The bottom one.'

We both cross the room to where Lizzie tugs on a dangling cord.

'Damn. Forgot about the power,' she says when the light bulb above us remains unlit. She switches on the torch feature on her phone instead.

The stream of light cuts through the darkness, taking away some of the sinister vibes of the place. I sigh, feeling a little more relaxed as Lizzie crouches down in front of me and rifles through the contents of the cupboard before bringing out a small box. We both peer inside and I'm relieved to see about ten or so neatly packed white candles.

'This should last us the night,' Lizzie says, sounding as relived as I feel. She hands me the dust-coated box and reaches in for another smaller box, a red one, which I recognise as the truth or dare card game we played ten years ago. Just seeing it makes my stomach churn.

A great gust of wind blows dried leaves and white sand down the steps, and I shiver.

'Remember these?' Lizzie asks.

I try to gauge whether she is being sarcastic or not, but her face is soft, and her tone doesn't imply any nastiness.

'Yeah, I remember,' I say. 'But I'd rather not.'

Lizzie stares at them in her hand for a while before she nods and closes the cupboard. Surely she doesn't expect us, grown adults, to play a juvenile game like truth or dare?

'Hey, did you notice anything weird about Tamara?' Lizzie asks, as she walks over to the generator and gives it a once-over. She touches something with her finger and then grimaces when she sees dark grease caked on her finger.

'No, what do you mean?'

'You know, the boobs... the hair...'

I shrug and wipe away the damp strands of hair stuck to my face with my free hand. 'She looks great. I mean, as long as she's happy, right?'

Lizzie wipes her dirty fingertip on an old oil rag. 'I have no beef with surgery. It's not that. It's just that she looks... so... like you now.'

I tilt my head. 'Do you really think so? That's weird. Lance mentioned something like that after he met her.'

'Don't you think she's starting to look a lot like you?'

I shrug, trying to hide my irritation at the comparison. 'Sure, if big boobs is all that I am to everyone, then yeah, she looks like me.'

Lizzie chuckles. 'No, silly. It's not just the boobs, it's the hair. She's grown it long like yours, right to her bum. And she's dyed it literally the exact shade of dark brown you have.' Lizzie loses the smile and shakes her head. 'I think it's a bit weird, to be honest.'

I shiver. This doesn't feel good. I'm not sure that I like what Lizzie's implying. I also don't care for the way she's trying to create something out of what is likely nothing. Tamara is my friend. And don't all woman experience insecurity about their bodies at some stage in their lives?

'Okay. Well. We've got the candles so let's go,' I say, giving the box a little shake and moving towards the staircase. I just want to get out of here.

Lance springs to mind. It's funny. I never imagined myself thinking this after all the hurt he's put me through with his cheating and lying, but I desperately want him to rescue me right this minute, and whisk me away from this basement, from this holiday house, from these people who were once my closest friends but are now strangers, from this part of my life that I want to keep buried.

Nothing about this weekend feels right anymore. To hell with processing and healing. Maybe Will thinks the track isn't crossable because he and Lizzie arrived in a fancy Lexus. But Lance's little Subaru is an all-wheel drive. He always brags about how well his car tackles slippery roads, and while I know all-out flooding is completely different to a shallow puddle here and there, we might still be able to make it across.

Another gust of wind blows down the steps, teasing the long, dark, strands of my hair across my face. Something tinkles from the dark corner of the room, where the little wooden table used to be. I look up and spy a wind chime swinging in the wind and reflecting the light from Lizzie's phone.

'Sienna sent me that. About two years after what happened. She said it'll spiritually cleanse the area.' Lizzie raises her brows. 'I don't usually believe in all that crap. But' – she shrugs – 'I feel like it helped. Maybe because I wanted it to. I don't get that skin-crawling feeling anymore when I'm down here.'

Speak for yourself, I think, the hairs on the back of my neck standing on end.

Lizzie turns off the torch feature on her phone which leaves us standing in the dim light coming from the trapdoor. I glance up and see the bruised clouds and my scalp prickles.

I give the box I'm holding another little shake, rattling the candles against each other. 'Let's get back upstairs. Come on.'

Lizzie narrows her gaze at me. In the dull, grey light, she looks almost ghostly in her white dress, and so painfully skinny, her cheekbones jutting out sharply. It honestly makes me so sad to see her this way. She's obviously still suffering from the loss of her dad, and likely still hasn't healed after what happened here ten years ago.

'So what's up with you and Lance? I sense something… it's as though you both…'

'We're fine,' I say, marching towards the stairs, feeling annoyed now. For a second there I was honestly going to reach out, offer an olive branch and ask Lizzie if she's okay. Because it's clear that she's not. But right now I just want to get away from her.

'Well, I'd keep a close eye on him if I were you. You wouldn't want someone, one of your own friends to go behind your back and betray you.'

'Why would anyone do that?' I ask, unable to suppress a shiver travelling from my head to my toes.

'Because they're a terrible friend.' Lizzie presses her lips together and shakes her head. 'It's the worst form of betrayal, isn't it? Stealing your friend's man?'

My face heats beneath the scrutiny of Lizzie's gaze. 'I'm going up.'

I take the stairs, my heart racing, but when I get about two thirds of the way up, Lizzie reaches out and grabs my arm, her fingers sinking into my bicep. I'm grateful, in this moment, that she doesn't wear those hideously pointy acrylic nails anymore. But still, my heart panics and my pulse drums loudly in my head.

'Imagine how Angelica felt the moment she fell?' she says, ice in her voice. 'I think about it all the time.' Something in Lizzie's voice has changed now, there's a vulnerability there, and potential tears thickening her throat. But I don't dare turn around to look in case I lose my footing. 'I wish I knew what happened that night. I just wish I knew the truth,' she says.

I take a deep breath in a bid to calm myself. 'So do I. Poor Angelica. She didn't deserve to die like that.'

Lizzie lets me go and after I take a second to breathe and compose myself, I move quickly up the stairs. I can't get out of this basement fast enough.

The sky opens up as I emerge out of the basement so I run, the candles rattling in the box. But the rain obscures my vision because I slam straight into a long, sinewy body.

'Hey, where are you going in such a hurry?' Jake grips my shoulders to steady me, his single blue eye glinting at me. He shifts his gaze behind me and back, then releases me. 'What's that hole over there you just came out of?'

I don't bother answering him or check to see where Lizzie is. I run straight back to the house, my heart hammering against my chest, replaying Jake's words over and over in my head like a recording. How did he not know where the trapdoor leads? Didn't Tamara say that Jake and Lucas were helping Will in the basement with the generator a little while ago?

Someone isn't telling the truth, and I need to know why.

16

Then

I wake up in the dark, my heart squeezing in panic because, for a second, I don't know where I am. But when I take a deep breath to calm myself, the delicious, unmistakable scent of fish and chips sends my empty stomach growling.

As I sit up and rub my eyes, a vague memory of Brayden and Lizzie announcing they were going to drive into town to get some fish and chips while the others were fighting over who got to use the downstairs shower first flits through my mind – that is, everyone but Sienna who Brayden had tucked into bed to sleep off the booze. I must have decided to lie down for a bit too, even though I can't remember doing it.

My head is pounding and I'm dying of thirst, but at least the nausea I felt on the beach is gone. Then I remember the sun, how hot it was, and glance down at my arms and feel my face. I'm not as burnt as I initially thought while I was out on the beach. Maybe that hardcore layer of sunscreen helped after all.

The food smells so good I don't have to force myself to get up. I just roll out of bed and shuffle my way towards the kitchen, allowing my hunger to lead the way.

Everyone is gathered around the kitchen bench, some perched on stools and some standing around two open parcels of hot food. One of golden, battered pieces of fish and the other a mound of hot chips.

Oh. My. God. The sight of the food has me weak at the knees. I have to cling to the counter when I reach it because a wave of dizziness washes over me and my whole body goes all shaky. But right now I need to quench my thirst more than anything so I reach for the nearby bottle of lemonade and pour myself a tall glass right to the top.

'Hey, Maz,' says Samuel laughing, his eyes on my hair while I down the entire glass of lemonade in one go. 'Your hair…' He shakes his head, his eyes twinkling.

I grip the counter again because I'm practically swooning with Sam staring at me like this, with so much affection in his eyes. I know he only cares for me like a sister but damn, my heart can't take it.

'What's wrong with it?' I ask, gasping for breath and setting the empty glass on the counter. Oh God, I needed that drink. My hands fly to my hair, the source of Samuel's amusement, and inwardly I cringe at how bad I must look. Self-consciously, I begin finger-combing what feels like a rat's nest. How on earth did my hair get into such a mess in the space of a few hours?

'Here,' Sam says, getting up and sliding his stool my way.

The act is not lost on Tamara and Angelica, who watch my interaction with Samuel closely. My stomach flutters with anxiety. Has everyone been talking about me while I've been sleeping?

'Hey, Maz, you stripped naked and skinny-dipped,' Lizzie says, raising her brows suggestively. 'Brayden's got it all on his phone.'

'What?' Blood rushes to my face, and I drop the crispy piece of hot fish I'd been so excited to bite into, my appetite instantly gone.

Samuel shoves Brayden so hard that he goes flying across the room and lands against the double-door fridge with a thud, the chips he'd been holding in his hand scattering to the floor.

'What the fuck, Samuel?' he says, his cheeks turning red with rage.

Lizzie comes to stand between them. 'Settle down, animals. I was joking. There is no such video because it didn't happen.'

'Why would you say something like that?' Tamara shakes her head, her gaze narrowed on Lizzie. 'You should apologise to Maz.'

Lizzie bites her bottom lip and raises her brows at the suggestion. I don't believe I've ever heard Lizzie apologise to anyone for anything in her life.

I fold my arms across my chest as I watch Lizzie pop a chip into her mouth. After she chews and swallows, which seems to take forever, she comes to my side and gives me a quick side-hug.

'Aww, Maz knows I'm only mucking around.' She glares at all the others. 'I mean, that's what we came down for, right? Fun? You know, *f...u...n*, fun? Ever heard of it, people?'

There are groans and sighs and then grunts of agreement. The tense moment has passed. Even Samuel and Brayden are bro-hugging each other.

After we demolish the fish and chips, forgetting to save some for Sienna in our post-drunken hunger, Tamara and I help Lizzie clean up while the boys set up drinks in the living room where we're going to hang out for most of the night. The view of the ocean at night, beneath the stars, is spectacular from there.

'I might make Sienna a quick salad. I feel bad she missed out on the fish and chips,' I say, opening the fridge and taking out a cold cooked chicken, a bag of lettuce and a container of cherry tomatoes.

'She probably won't even eat it. She's on another diet, remember?' says Tamara.

'What one this time?' Lizzie asks.

Tamara shrugs. 'I've only seen her drink lemon water out of her drink bottle.'

'So that's why she got so drunk. I mean, I can't talk. I was running so late this morning I forgot to eat breakfast.' I shrug.

'Here,' says Lizzie, opening a little green box on the counter and handing me two white pills. 'Paracetamol for your headache.'

'How d'you know I had a headache?'

She shrugs, her long blonde hair bouncing along with the gesture. She's had a shower since swimming and has washed all the salt from her hair, unlike me.

'You keep frowning like you're worried something bad is going to happen. Take those and lighten up.' Lizzie claps her hands together and smiles brilliantly. 'Now let's go party with the boys before they steal all our drinks.'

'Where's Angelica?' asks Samuel, who enters the kitchen just as I'm washing down my pills with half a glass of tap water.

'She's in her room,' says Tamara, looking offended that Samuel even asked. 'Writing a letter to some guy,' she adds, and I swear there's a self-satisfied gleam in her eye that I don't like the look of.

A dark look crosses Samuel's face. He shakes his head, grabs a beer from the fridge, then storms down the hallway to the front door and heads outside into the night, slamming the door behind him.

'What's up with your psycho best friend? He's been acting really creepy.' Lizzie shudders and locks her lavender eyes with mine. 'Maybe you should go talk to him before we all end up on the news as murder victims or something.'

Goosebumps prickle my arms. Didn't Lizzie just tell me to lighten up?

'Well,' I say, 'maybe you should ask your best friend, who's up there writing letters to some guy, to speak to Samuel and at least let him know what's going on.'

Lizzie pulls her head back as though I've slapped her, and I've never felt so satisfied, and a little frightened, to be honest, in my life.

'Angelica is doing nothing wrong. What she's doing is her business and nobody has a right to invade her privacy, including her boyfriend.'

I want to say so much more, but instead I groan with frustration and head to the fridge and grab myself a can of vodka and passionfruit.

'I'm going to find Samuel,' I say, the icy can numbing my fingers already.

When I step outside, I close the door quietly behind me even though I'd rather slam it like Samuel had done, then I crack open the can.

The drink goes down easily despite how shaky I'd felt earlier, the sugar giving me an extra boost of energy. By the time I've climbed the dunes, I'm tipping my head back to get the last drops out of the can. Done. I crunch the can in my hand and toss it on the edge of the path. I'll pick it up again on my way back to the house.

The water is stunning at night, breathtakingly so, the moon tinting the ocean and the shimmering shoreline silver. As I walk along the beach, I call out for Sam until my throat is hoarse, but he's nowhere to be seen.

Around ten minutes later, I hear the soft pad of footsteps in the dunes behind me and my heart leaps and I spin around.

'Tamara,' I say, unable to hide the disappointment in my voice. 'I thought you were Sam.'

'You still haven't found him?' She comes to stand beside me and scans the length of the beach, looking left and right and shaking her head, but then she stiffens. 'Oh my God.' She points to the water in front of us, her eyes wide. 'It's Samuel!'

I grip her arm and follow her gaze out to the glittering dark sea. 'Where?'

'There he is!' She points at something floating on the water, and when my eyes adjust, I feel sick.

There's a body floating out in the ocean.

And that body belongs to my best friend, Sam.

17

Now

'I couldn't find anything,' says Will, rubbing a towel all over his damp hair. He returned without the rest of the guys ten minutes ago, soaked to the bone and irritable after not having found the phone signal he was looking for.

'Yeah, I didn't think you would,' Lizzie says, looking unconcerned as she unwraps a huge round of Brie and places it at the centre of a square white platter. 'Trust me, I spent my entire teenage life trying to find a signal out here before my dad relented and got a landline so we could have Wi-Fi.' Lizzie shrugs. 'Some days you get lucky. But those are the blue-skied days, not the stormy ones.' She adjusts the Brie until it's perfectly centred, then looks up and widens her eyes slightly at Will. 'Um, don't you think it's time you took a shower?'

Will blinks, glances at me, then back at Lizzie. For a few seconds he stares at her, then he opens his mouth as though to speak, but instead abruptly turns away and heads upstairs.

Interesting. There is something amiss with Will and Lizzie's relationship. It's clear that Lizzie has all the control, but it's also obvious that Will doesn't like it.

And I thought Lance and I were going to be the weirdest couple here.

Speaking of Lance, I need to find him and ask if he can go see for himself, in his own car, if the track is crossable or not.

'Does anybody know where Lance is?' I ask.

Right on cue the front door opens and Lance and Jake burst in, completely soaked, their hair pasted to their faces and their clothes stuck to their bodies. The two men are chuckling, elbowing each other in a playful way. I guess I should be glad that at least someone is having fun.

I try not to rush to Lance's side as I don't want to bring any unnecessary attention my way. 'I need to speak with you,' I tell him, my voice lowered as I eye Jake who's watching us a little too closely. 'Alone.'

Lance kicks off his shoes and leaves them beside the doormat. 'Can I have a shower first?' He's trembling so hard his teeth rattle.

I frown at Jake and lean in closer still, standing on my tiptoes so that I can whisper in Lance's ear. 'We need to get out of here. Now.'

Lance nods at Jake, who, after kicking off his shoes, walks away, leaving us alone.

'Jake and I just drove out to see if my car could make it and it's a big fat no.' He leans in and strokes a lock of hair away from my cheek. 'We might be stuck here for a couple of days, at least.'

'Are you serious?' My heart takes a dive. There's got to be another way out of here. There is no way I'm going to be comfortable sleeping here tonight when I don't even know whom I can trust.

'Stop stressing.' Lance shakes his head. 'These people aren't that bad. We'll be okay, even if we do have to stay an extra night or two.'

'Hey, Maz, will you run up and get those glasses you and Lance had earlier? I need to wash 'em so we have enough for dinner.' Lizzie tears open a packet of breadsticks and stacks them onto the platter beside the Brie.

'I'll go,' says Lance, looking relieved to have an excuse to get away from me. 'I'm going up for a shower anyway.'

Lizzie turns to us. 'No. Don't!'

Lance and I stare at Lizzie, surprised by the harshness of her outburst. Her cheeks tint pink. 'Will is in the shower and when both are used up there it can screw up the hot water system. You'll have to wait, Lance.' Lizzie smiles sweetly at him. 'There are towels in the linen cupboard.' She wipes her hands on a tan-coloured tea towel and points towards the back of the house at the laundry door. 'You can dry off in there while you wait.'

Lance mutters something under his breath and squelches his way down the hallway towards the laundry.

'The glasses please,' says Lizzie, nodding towards the staircase.

'Sure,' I say, feeling grateful to have an excuse to disappear for a few minutes as I climb the stairs.

But just when I'm about to enter the bedroom, Will calls out to me from Lizzie's parents' room.

'Hey, Marilyn. Can you come help me please? I can't work out how the digital temperature control works in the shower.'

'Oh… okay.' I try to keep my eyes focused on his face and not on the towel wrapped loosely around his naked hips. 'I'm not sure that I'll be of any use though.' Why does he think I'm going to be any help? He should be asking Lizzie, not me. Still, I follow him into the ensuite bathroom and give it a go, tapping at the keys.

'Hmm, I'm not sure what's wrong with it.' I shrug. 'I'm hopeless with technology, sorry. I'll call Lance.'

'No. Wait. There's something… I need to ask you.'

My heart races as Will steps into the shower cubicle with me, bringing with him the piney scent of his aftershave. He's a great-looking guy. Someone that could easily be found on a magazine cover or a catwalk. But being in such small quarters with him, even though it's a double shower so larger than usual, is making me feel slightly uncomfortable.

'You seem like a great girl, Marilyn,' he says, his dark gaze on mine. 'You're beautiful too. Lance is a lucky man.'

'Oh. We're actually not–' I stop myself. Why am I confiding in Will? I don't even know the guy. 'Sorry, but I need to get some wine glasses for Lizzie.'

Will shuffles in closer and dips his head to meet my gaze. 'You're actually not what?'

'Nothing,' I say, dropping my gaze and noticing that the towel is coming loose. 'Forget... um, forget I even said it.'

I've always thought that women are different from men. That we need to get to know a guy in order to find him attractive, whereas men can find women attractive upon first sight. I've just proven myself wrong. Will is insanely attractive. But it doesn't mean I want to be trapped in the confines of a bathroom with him, in his girlfriend's house.

Will folds his arms across his broad, tanned chest and takes a half-step back to allow me a little breathing space. 'Does Lance treat you right? I get the feeling he doesn't.'

When I look up to meet Will's gaze, I can see sympathy there. It's odd. One minute it feels like he's trying to have a crack at me and the next he's being gentle and understanding.

'He cheated on me. Multiple times. But the multiple is on me, because I should have walked away after the first time.' There, I said it. I'm not sure why. But it feels... good, to get it all off my chest. Up until this moment,

Lance and I, along with his mystery ladies, were the only ones who knew about his infidelities.

Will nods and then he sucks in a huge breath and licks his lips.

'Do you ever feel like getting revenge?'

I take a step back and accidentally kick the glass shower door. It rattles so loudly but comes to an abrupt halt when I press my palm against the cool, smooth surface.

'What do you mean?'

'I mean...' Will pauses and sighs, rubs the back of his neck with what appears to be a trembling hand. He looks just about as uncomfortable as I feel right now. So why is he doing this? Why is he propositioning me? 'If you want to... get back at him, well... I'm happy to be that man.'

My pulse blows up in my ears. Did he really just say that?

'Wait. So you'd hurt Lizzie just to help me get revenge?' I shake my head. Great. Just when I think I've unearthed an understanding, sympathetic guy. 'You're just as bad as he is. And let me pass,' I say, barging past him and stepping out of the shower.

'Wait. Marilyn.' Will swears to himself. 'I'm not usually like this, just please, please let me explain.'

But I get the hell out of that bedroom before he gets the chance.

18

'I love this. It's so… full of flavour,' I say, raising the strip of grilled chicken on my fork. I've had way too much wine, and I'm babbling nonsense because I can't bear the awkward silence at dinner any longer.

The storm seems to have passed, but the heavy rain looks to be settling in all night. It's almost cosy inside the house, with the warm, flickering glow of the candlelight at the centre of the table. Almost. The frostiness between us all sitting around the table is enough to keep the warm camaraderie at bay.

'It's just chicken,' says Lizzie, rolling her lavender eyes. 'I just chucked it in the pan and it grilled itself. Anyone can do it.'

Will raises his eyes to the ceiling and throws me a glance of sympathy. I'm puzzled by Will's behaviour at the table. He's been making polite chit-chat and giving me eye contact without looking away or being embarrassed by what occurred earlier. It's almost as though he's not embarrassed or bothered by my rebuff in any way. He seems pleased. Friendlier towards me even. It's strange.

Although I didn't tell Lizzie, or anyone for that matter, what happened between Will and me upstairs, she's been extra hostile towards me. Lizzie also seems to be ignoring Will, which makes me wonder if she has secret cameras in all the rooms of the house, including the bathrooms, and she's been watching us all. That isn't exactly far-fetched. With the kind of money Lizzie's family have, it's entirely possible.

Once we've eaten, Jake and Lucas clear the table, and Lizzie smiles for the first time all evening.

'Maz and I found something in the basement.' She places the small red box on the table and I immediately tense up. 'Truth or dare. Remember when we played this? Maz? You should remember. It's the night you chose to kiss Brayden instead of the guy you were truly obsessed with. You know, the guy who died. Your best friend. Sam.'

The entire table falls silent.

'That's a low blow, Lizzie, and you know it,' Tamara says, her voice low. She shakes her head, her gaze fixed on the little red box as though she wants to throw it on the ground and stomp on it until she obliterates it.

Lance looks at Tamara and then I can feel his eyes on me. He's wanted to know about what happened for so long and now he's finally getting some information.

Lucas shifts in his seat and rubs the back of his shirt collar before pushing his chair back and getting up.

'I'm tired. I've had a long week. So count me out.' He leaves the table and disappears down the hallway.

Sienna eyes us all while she gnaws on her bottom lip before she stands. 'I think I'll join Lucas. Sorry.' She rushes out of the room before anybody can object. I can imagine Sienna and Lucas lying in bed together and whispering about leaving tomorrow as soon as the track dries up.

I'm about to nudge Lance with my elbow and suggest we go upstairs – I'd rather we spend the night hanging out together in the bedroom, chatting or even reading a book than sitting here with strangers and my old friends, who may as well be strangers – but then I catch Lizzie glaring at me from across the table and it irritates me to no end.

'Actually, let's play truth or dare,' I say, my heart pounding wildly. 'Maybe there are some things that need to be said. Things about the past. Maybe the truth needs to come out, and maybe then we can finally put it all behind us.'

Tamara stands up abruptly, her lips pressed together, and knocks the table so that her empty wine glass falls off the edge and smashes to the floor.

'You guys can sit here and dredge up the past all you like, but I'm not interested. It happened. It was a tragedy. Talking about it is not going to change anything or bring them back.' She shakes her head and I can see her cheeks growing pink with rage. 'To think I actually thought this weekend was going to be fun.' She takes a careful step back and bends to pick up the broken glass, but then sucks in a sharp breath and swears, nursing a bleeding thumb. 'Oh shit.'

'Are you okay?' I ask.

'Come on, Jake,' she says, ignoring me and tugging on Jake's shirtsleeve, rage flaring in her cheeks. 'Let's go to bed.'

Jake turns his head so that he meets my eyes with his single one. He remains seated. 'I'd actually like to hear about what happened here… all those years ago,' he says.

At this, Tamara storms off in a huff. Seconds later, she slams their bedroom door shut.

'Tamara never likes to talk about it.' Jake shrugs, his one blue eye bright and piercing. 'It makes her upset and, to be honest, it makes her angry. She gets all… filled with hate. But I would like to know what happened, from another perspective… so that I can help her through it.'

'You and me both,' says Lance. He tips his head back and finishes the rest of his beer.

'Who does she hate?' I ask. 'Has she ever said anything to you about it?'

Jake's one eye pierces through my soul. 'Maybe if you tell me exactly what happened I can answer your question.'

'This is getting too heavy for me,' says Will. He widens his dark eyes at Lizzie who is staring at the candle at the centre of the table, her eyes transfixed on the flame, then shakes his head. 'I'm going to bed.'

Lizzie doesn't even flinch or glance at him. I'm not sure that she even notices him leaving the table.

That's the strange thing about Lizzie and Will. Although they are boyfriend and girlfriend, I've seen no evidence of intimacy, or even a sense of closeness between them. But then again they could be one of those couples that only do intimacy behind closed doors.

I reach for my wine glass but realise that it's empty. How many glasses have I had now, five… maybe six? At that thought my head starts to spin and I reach for my water glass and bring it to my lips. Oh God, what am I doing here? Why did I come to this place? I knew I should never have let Lance drive me down. Maybe my car breaking down was a sign not to go, a sign I should have taken notice of.

Oh well. I take a huge glug of water and spill some down my white top, but I don't even bother to get up and get changed. A wet top is the least of my problems. I really need to leave this place and get my life back on track. As soon as we get home, I'm giving Lance three days to move out. I cannot live this way any longer, clinging to him out of fear. It's time to move on.

From everything.

'Yeah, Maz,' says Lizzie, blinking herself out of the trance.

She tops up her wine glass and fills mine to the brim. A drop of red slides down the side of my glass and drips onto the jarrah tabletop. It looks like blood and reminds me of the blood on the basement floor, pooling around Angelica's head.

'Maybe you can tell us all what happened ten years ago.' Lizzie's hand trembles as she raises the wine to her lips and takes a sip. 'I mean, after all, you're the one who found the bodies.'

19

Then

'Where were you three?' Lizzie stands at the front door, narrowing her gaze at Tamara, Samuel and me. 'You guys have been gone for ages. We've been waiting.'

'Out for a walk,' I say as casually as I can, brushing beach sand from my legs and ankles before I step inside. 'Sam had a swim but Tamara and I just waded in for a bit. The water's pretty cold.'

Samuel exhales and gives me a grateful smile as he enters the house and my heart warms. Of course I'd never tell the others what happened and especially what he'd confessed, words that broke my heart, words that he whispered only to me, after Tamara and I rushed into the water and dragged him from the moonlit sea to the safety of the shore.

'Well, grab a towel and come join us in the living room as we're about to play truth or dare.'

Tamara and I follow Lizzie into the living area where the others are laughing about something Brayden said.

Sienna takes a sip from her can and giggles again. 'God, you're an idiot, I can't believe we're related.'

She hurls a pillow at his head and he ducks. It knocks over a wooden sculpture which makes Lizzie gasp.

'Oi, settle down,' Lizzie says, coming to ruffle the back of Brayden's hair. She sits opposite him on the other side of the coffee table, next to Angelica, who is pouring Lizzie a shot of vodka.

Lizzie knocks back the vodka and places a small box at the centre of the glass table and lifts the lid then takes out a pack of cards with 'Truth or Dare' emblazoned on the back in bold red letters.

Lizzie's threat from earlier comes back to haunt me and I immediately feel sick. Maybe I should lie and say the sushi gave me food poisoning and go hide my shame in the bedroom. But then that would give everyone the opportunity to talk behind my back and make their own assumptions on my feelings for Samuel. Urgh. Then Samuel would find out and I'd never be able to look him in the eye again. He'll likely shun me.

No. It's better that I sit here and lie my way through the game. Or just choose dare. Anyway, hopefully Samuel takes his time getting dried off.

'Okay, I'll go first.' Lizzie selects a card, and her lavender eyes fix on me. 'Maz, truth or dare?'

'Dare,' I say, just as Samuel enters the room and sits down in the space between Tamara and me, a fluffy white towel around his neck and shoulders. I try to keep my body relaxed and my face as unbothered as possible but it's difficult when Lizzie is focusing on you.

Lizzie's perfectly manicured eyebrows shoot up as she reads the instructions on the card. 'Okay, Maz.' She throws her head back and laughs. 'You're going to love this one.' Lizzie makes eye contact with Samuel and winks, then rests her twinkly-eyed gaze on me. 'Marilyn, your dare is to tongue-kiss the person you find the most attractive.'

My stupid eyes immediately seek out Samuel, who is staring down at his drink, his dark hair still wet from the ocean. He looks uncomfortable. Oh God. My face heats up the more Lizzie laughs.

'Go on. Kiss someone. You've got about five more seconds, or you drink this entire glass of straight bourbon in one go.'

Lizzie slides the glass at the centre of the table my way, some of the bourbon spilling over the brim and wetting the table. Just the smell of it turns my stomach after today's drinking session on the beach.

Brayden is sitting on the other side of me, so without thinking about it for too long, I force myself to turn away from Samuel and face Brayden instead. I try my hardest to ignore the smug look on Brayden's face, and the gasps and shouts from the others as I lean in to kiss him.

'Oh my God!' Sienna cries, as Brayden groans and eagerly responds to my half-hearted kiss by gripping the back of my neck so that I can't escape as he spears his tongue down my throat.

He tastes like bourbon and the weird barbeque-rib-flavoured potato chips he's been eating, and his tongue is swirling mine around so vigorously I'm worried I'm going to get a cramp. When he finally releases his hand from my neck, I fall away from him, bumping against Samuel and gasping for breath. I feel like I've just survived a tornado.

'There's more of that later if you want it,' Brayden says with a wink, as I'm wiping my wet mouth.

Lizzie leans over the table and lightly whacks the side of his head but she's laughing. Brayden is only her plaything for the week, so it's not like she truly cares for him deeply or anything, but I do think she's maybe a little annoyed that he got into the kiss so much.

I take a long gulp of my second can of vodka and lemonade, and another, until I can no longer taste Brayden. Then I glance sideways and meet Samuel's eyes. He smiles at me, sadly, like he feels sorry for me. Urgh. Pity. Great.

'Your turn,' Lizzie says, raising her brows.

I sigh and pick up a card.

'Choose someone.'

I shrug and choose Angelica, who keeps staring down into her phone. She looks up, blinking several times. 'What?'

'Maybe get off your phone and concentrate,' Tamara mutters beneath her breath.

Yikes. I need to get her alone and tell her to chill as her hostility towards Angelica is going overboard.

'We're playing truth or dare,' says Sienna, smiling kindly at Angelica who puts her phone away in the back pocket of her jeans.

'Oh, okay.' Angelica looks at me expectantly.

'Truth or dare?' I ask.

'Truth?'

I nod. This is where I could be a real bitch and say, 'Who is Cameron?' but I don't. Because I guess it's none of my business who she's writing to. And anyway, Sam told me the guy's name in secret, so I don't want to get him into trouble. Not that it's much of a secret anymore. I think everyone here knows about it, even if they're pretending that they don't.

'Are you in love with Samuel?' I suppose this one is none of my business either but it's what popped up in my head and with everyone eyeballing me, my nerves got to me and I just blurted it out as opposed to choosing something a little less intense.

Angelica glances at Samuel, then at Lizzie who nods as though she's approving Angelica giving her answer. It's ridiculous how much sway Lizzie has on everyone in the group. We all need to grow our own spines, me especially.

'I really care about Samuel. But we haven't said "I love you" to each other yet. Samuel told me that we need to say it when we truly mean it.'

Samuel blushes as all eyes turn to him.

'So you don't love my best friend?' Lizzie asks, frowning. 'But you're a stage-five clinger. I thought you would have said it on the first date,' she says, rolling her eyes. 'Boring. Okay. Next.'

She slides the little stack of cards towards Angelica, who selects one.

'Tamara,' Angelica says. 'Truth or dare?'

'Truth.'

'Why don't we hang out as much as we used to? You and me, we used to be tight.' She smiles sadly at Tamara, whose head is down.

Finally Tamara looks up and shrugs, and I'm surprised to see that her eyes are glazed over with tears. 'I'm not sure why. I think you got super close with Lizzie and... sometimes it's hard to be noticed when Lizzie is around.'

'Okay, blame me for your inadequacies.' Lizzie rolls her eyes.

Tamara sighs. 'You're right. Sorry. That was wrong. I guess I am insecure. You guys are so beautiful, and funny and... sometimes I just feel a little bit invisible.'

'But you're fine with Maz,' says Lizzie. 'Is that because you think she's bland and not beautiful and funny? Does being around her boost your ego?'

Samuel stands up, his eyes narrowed at Lizzie. 'That's way out of line and you know it.' He rakes a hand through his damp hair and shakes his head. 'I'm going for a walk.'

He takes one last look at Angelica before he leaves, perhaps hoping that she'll follow. But she doesn't.

'This game sucks. How about we play strip poker?' suggests Brayden.

'Yes!' says Lizzie.

'Eww,' says Sienna. 'I'm not stripping in front of my brother.'

'Well, look away or go to bed, little girl' – Brayden winks at Lizzie – 'because us big people are going to get naked.'

'Well, I'm out of here,' says Sienna, getting up.

The others laugh.

'I'm going to go check on Sam,' I say, casting a glance at Angelica in case she decides she'd rather go. But she continues to stare down at her hands, picking at her cuticles. She's probably thinking about Cameron. Oh God, I'm turning into Tamara. I shake my head and get up.

As soon as I step outside, a cool breeze tickles my bare arms and legs, giving me goosebumps. I regret not putting on a jumper first.

'Sam?' I call out, as I walk over the dunes to get to the wet, foamy shore. My heart flutters in panic as I think about what he told me after Tamara and I dragged him from the water.

'Hey,' he calls out from my right, where there's a little dip in the sand dunes by the bush, the moonlight illuminating half of his face.

As I get closer, I can see that he's been crying.

'Samuel. Are you okay?' I ask, reaching out to touch his arm.

He swallows and looks out across the silvery sea, rubbing at his eyes with the flat of his palm.

'Tell me what's wrong, please, Sam. Tell me what's making you so sad.'

Sam swallows and raises his head to the silvery light of the moon, his eyes closed, then nods.

'I'll try, Maz. But I don't know if you'll understand.'

20

Now

'We're waiting.' Lizzie folds her arms across her chest and sighs. 'Come on, Maz, it's about time you told us.'

Lance and Jake watch me closely. The air in the room has become thick and intense. I don't want to do this. But if I don't, then this weekend will be all for nothing and I'll still have the past hanging around my neck like a ball and chain, dragging me down for the rest of my life. I need to end this now. Tell everyone what happened, or at least, my part.

'It was the worst night of my life.' I take a sip of wine in a bid to calm my nerves, but my hand trembles so much that a splash of red spills over the edge, dripping down my hand. I pass the glass into my other hand so that I can suck the wine off my fingers, and I end up spilling half of it onto my lap.

I gasp and stand up, grabbing one of the napkins from dinner and start blotting my jeans but it's no use. This will stain, badly. But that's the least of my problems. In fact, it gives me an excuse to go upstairs and get myself together while I get changed into some clean clothes.

'You did that on purpose.' Lizzie shakes her head. 'You're hiding something from us, I just know it.'

'Leave her alone,' says Lance. 'She's going to get changed and then she's going to come back down and tell us everything, aren't you, Maz?'

I look at Lance and he gives me a look, a 'you can do this' look and I nod.

'I'll be back. And I will tell you everything. I promise.'

'Sure you will,' says Lizzie sarcastically.

I ignore Lizzie and address the boys. 'I'll be back in five.'

I wipe my hand and the wine glass with the cloth before taking my wine with me upstairs. Five minutes will at least give me enough time to talk myself into this, psych myself up. At least I don't need time to plan what I'm going to say, because what happened has been etched into my mind these past ten years.

Warm light flickers from the corner of the room where Lizzie placed a candle in a jar earlier, giving the room a cosy feel. I sit on the edge of the bed and sip my wine, looking through and past my reflection as I gaze out the window and watch the waves thrash about in the ferocious wind as lightning dances across the sky. It's like watching a heavy metal music video come to life.

After I drain my glass, I feel better, but sleepy, and less enthusiastic about going back downstairs and spilling my guts onto the table for everyone to see. If I could curl up on my bed and call it a night I would. Even better, I'd stay in here until the track dries up and then somehow develop parkour skills and jump out the window and run straight to Lance's car without ever seeing anyone again. But then I remember that I don't have a manual licence so I'd need Lance for that. Plus, I can't exactly abandon him when he came all the way down here on this trip for me.

A quick glance at the bedside clock tells me I've spent ten minutes up here. I suppose I should be getting back downstairs now. Nerves flutter in my belly and my heart races just to know that they are waiting for me. I wonder if I should take one of my anxiety relief pills. Hopefully they still work with all this alcohol swimming in my veins.

I set my wine glass down on Lance's bedside table and then roll across the bed to get my pills from my own table, but when I reach out for my toiletry bag, I find a piece of paper draped across it.

I pick it up and when I see what it is, I freeze.

It's a printout of a photo, on A4 paper, that I swear wasn't there earlier today, and I recognise the moment captured on film, and the two people in the photo on the beach.

Because it's me and Samuel, and it's a moment I'll never forget.

With trembling fingers I carefully hold the picture and stare at it, drinking in all the details of Sam's face.

My heart aches at the memory of this moment and at the same time, I'm glad to see it. Because it confirms to me that it did happen. That it wasn't just a romanticised version of the true events. This *was* the true event.

Samuel has his hands resting on my waist and he's staring into my eyes smiling, clearly happy. This is the very moment he discovered that I had feelings for him. Because I'll never forget the look on his face when I told him.

My blood runs cold as I drag my eyes away from Samuel's beautiful face to read the words typed across the top of the picture.

I WAS THERE

The hairs on the back of my neck prickle as I realise that this photo exists because somebody took it while we were unawares. They invaded our privacy.

But who here would do this? Who would take this old photo and print a copy of it on A4 paper and leave it here for me to see? A sick and twisted individual, that's who.

The obvious person is Lizzie. She's the one who invited me here. It's just too coincidental. This entire weekend has been planned out, carefully, by whoever has left this photo here for me to find, and Lizzie is the only one whom I can imagine coming up with something like this. Tamara and Sienna wear their hearts on their sleeves and are too easily read. This is definitely Lizzie's work.

Maybe Lizzie set this whole thing up because she blames me for what happened? Could she have said something to Lance earlier when they were alone? Something that frightened him enough to want us to leave immediately earlier in the day? He has been more insistent in wanting to know what happened here since his time alone with Lizzie.

A lump forms in my throat as I stare at Sam's slightly blurred features. What I wouldn't give to jump into this photo and relive this moment. I'd change what I said to him. Not because my words held no truth or meaning, but because they held too much truth and ultimately led to my best friend's demise.

I blink away my tears and feel a rage ignite in my belly. At myself mostly. But also at whoever left this photo here for me to find. How dare they play games over something that is so painful to me, and to everyone else involved? If someone wants to confront me about this, then they need to do it face to face. I'm happy to come clean. I'm happy to relieve myself of this horrible burden.

I push myself up from the bed and storm downstairs, picture in hand, my face throbbing with heat and my heart pounding furiously against my ribcage.

'Who did this?' I demand, when I enter the dining room, waving the photo in front of me.

Lizzie stares at me blankly. 'Did what?'

I sigh in frustration. 'This!' I slam the picture on the table in front of her and when she sees it she freezes, her eyes widening.

'Where did you find this?'

'In my room, on my bedside table. It wasn't there before.' I throw a glance at Lance who shrugs and shows his palms as if to say, 'don't ask me'.

'Pass it here,' Lance says to Lizzie, who is holding it with trembling fingers.

She ignores him so he stands to get a better look at it over her shoulder. 'That's you, Maz… and… some guy.'

'What the hell is going on?' Tamara has emerged from her room, rubbing at her eyes, her bare feet slapping against the polished floor. 'Some of us are trying to get some sleep.'

Sienna also appears, followed by Lucas, looking as though neither had even attempted sleep and were simply avoiding us all. I don't blame them.

'What's happening?' Lucas asks, his arms wrapped protectively around Sienna.

Lizzie hands Tamara the piece of paper and Tamara's face pales at first, then it turns red and her hands begin to shake. At first I think it's the emotional impact of seeing Samuel's face after all these years, but then she lifts her head and narrows her gaze at me.

'So you did sneak around with Samuel behind Angelica's back,' Tamara says, looking as though she could kill me. 'Did you do something to Angelica when you realised that Sam didn't want you? I bet you were the one who killed her.'

I'm so thrown by Tamara's outburst that my throat clams up and I can't speak.

'Unbelievable,' she says, shaking her head as though my silence confirms her theory.

'He did want me,' I finally say, my voice tight. 'And I didn't push Angelica. She was my friend. How could you even think that I'd do such a thing? I cared about them both.'

'That's what you want us to think, don't you?' Lizzie says, getting up to stand beside Tamara. Suddenly the two are teaming up against me.

Sienna clears her throat. 'Wait. There's something I have to tell you all.'

She looks at me, her dark eyes wide while she wrings her hands. 'I took that photo of you and Samuel.'

'You were in the bushes that night?' I ask.

She nods. 'Yeah. And I heard everything you two said.'

21

Sienna sighs and drops into the nearest chair. We all watch in silence as she pours herself a large glass of red.

'I was lying on my back watching the stars behind some bushes. I wanted privacy because I'd been sick and was worried I was going to do it again all over Lizzie's parents' nice floor. Then you guys moved back a little closer to my secret spot and I couldn't leave. So I sat there and listened while you talked. Then… after I heard what you guys said, I had to take a look at you both, to see if what I was hearing was real.' Sienna shrugs and nods at the photo. 'I saw this exact moment, and it was actually so beautiful I had to take a picture. But after what happened… not long after this was taken, I made a point to never show anyone. Because I didn't want to cause any trouble. I still don't.'

'So are you saying you didn't print this out and leave it for me to find?' I ask.

Lance makes a sound in his throat when Sienna shakes her head emphatically.

'What?' Sienna sits forward in her seat and glares at Lance. I've never seen her so riled before. 'Do you have a problem with me?'

Lance makes a face at Sienna and shakes his head. 'Why would I? I don't even know you.'

When his gaze rests on the picture of Sam and me, a sneer forms on his lips. 'I guess this photo explains a lot.' Lance finally meets my gaze, his hazel eyes glowing with hostility. 'So this guy's the reason why you can't even form a proper connection with me, and from your reaction to seeing his face again, it's pretty obvious you still hold a candle for him.'

'Don't be ridiculous.'

Lance's hands, which are resting against the tabletop, make fists. Sometimes he gets like this when he's drunk. Ridiculously jealous. He once kept me up all night, ranting and raving about how I've built walls around my heart, all because I refused to tell him the name of the first person I ever fell in love with.

'Where is he now? Why didn't he come this weekend?' Lance laughs. It's not a pleasant sound. 'He's lucky that he's not here, because if he were, I'd punch his fucking face in.'

I'm about to go mental at Lance and tell him to shut up and that his ego can go to hell, but Tamara clears her throat and leans across the table, her eyes blazing at Lance.

'You can't punch him in the face, dickhead. Unless you have a time travel machine.' Tamara shakes her head as her eyes film over with tears. 'He's dead. Samuel died ten years ago.' She wipes a tear from her cheek and looks at me before she shakes her head and storms off.

Lizzie gets up and disappears into the kitchen only to return with a bottle of gin. 'I think we all need a stiff drink.' She pours me one and slides it my way. 'Drink that and then we're talking. I need to know exactly what happened between you and Samuel. I've always thought something was off about that night. I felt something in the air, and I could tell that something wasn't right with Samuel.'

I want to tell her that Samuel was happy that night. But I'd be lying if I said that. Because even though he was radiant with joy, his eyes bright with excitement the last time I saw him, I can't deny that only hours earlier, Samuel, my beautiful best friend, had tried to drown himself in the sea.

'You need to tell us everything, Maz.' Lizzie absentmindedly traces the scar on her head with trembling fingers then looks me straight in the eye. 'I want to know why my best friend died that night.'

I take the shot and bring it to my lips. The gin tingles against my tongue, but when I swallow, it leaves a trail of fire running down my throat and into my belly, giving me some well-needed fuel and courage.

All eyes are on me as the wind howls outside and blows against this monstrous house, whistling at us through the cracks.

'Okay. I'll tell my truth. But I think *everyone* needs to be honest about that night. If I talk, we all talk.'

22

Then

'I don't know. I don't know what's wrong with me.' Samuel sighs deeply and shakes his head. When he meets my gaze, it breaks my heart to see the fresh tears in his eyes. 'I just don't feel right. I've been feeling strange lately. Bleak. Everything makes me sad.'

'Is it the Angelica thing? The letters?'

He nods and sways on his feet for a moment before he starts walking towards the shore. I follow, staying close to his side. Sam and Brayden have been drinking rum and cola since we came in from the beach earlier today. The last I looked the bottle had only about a quarter left in it and I'd say a large portion of it is swimming through Sam's veins as we speak.

'Partly... the fact that she's writing to some guy does make me sad. But it's not that... it's... other things... things I'd normally be able to handle... but can't anymore. The old me would say, oh well, she's got another guy on the side, man up, end it and move on. I mean, she's a great girl. But I'm not in love with her. She's not in love with me either. We're just... two people who like hanging out. I care about her a lot, of course, but... it's not like I'm going to crumble if she ends up with this Cameron guy.'

Cool water tickles my feet when we reach the shore and I gasp. Samuel doesn't flinch. We walk for a little bit, but we don't get very far because Sam is sluggish.

'So why don't you just break up?'

Samuel frowns and lifts his head to stare out across the glittering sea. 'Because… I feel so fucking lonely, you know? Like I need her. I don't know… I just need someone.'

A lone gull circles us then lands on the sea, where it bobs on the moonlit surface.

'You've got me. You've always got me, Sammy,' I say, using the childhood nickname he only allows me to call him.

His chin, and his entire jaw stiffens at this, and he stifles a sob and turns away from me, his shoulders hunched. 'Don't say things like that to me, Maz.' Sam heads back towards the dunes.

'Why not?' I ask, following him, my heart pounding as I reach out and touch his back ever so gently. Samuel's skin burns hot beneath his thin shirt and his body trembles at my touch.

'Because it makes me think… it gives me…' He rubs at his eyes angrily. 'Ah… crap, look, don't worry. It's the booze talking. I've drunk way too much today. I should have stopped at the vodka.'

My pulse hammers against my skull.

'Am I making you uncomfortable?' I say, removing my hand from his back.

Oh God. All this time Sam has been disgusted by my affections for him. I give him the creeps. That's what he wanted to say.

'I'm sorry if I've ever made you feel creeped out. I didn't mean… I've never meant for any of this to happen. It's just… you're such a beautiful guy, the most amazing person I've ever met and… yeah, I'm sorry. I'm so sorry.'

Samuel whips around and stares at me, his wet lashes stuck together making little dark triangles, his eyes wide. He gently places his warm hands on my arms, and I feel unsteady at the feel of his touch.

'Wait. What are you trying to say, Maz?'

I look him in the eye. This is the moment that I should lie, keep my secret, but I don't. Because I'm so sick of hiding my feelings. Even if it means I may lose him, at least he'll know.

'That I've kind of... been in love with you... for a long time. Again, I'm sorry,' I say, feeling more alive than I have in a long time and not sorry in the slightest. I'm not sorry because Samuel is the most amazing person I have ever met in my life and I'm glad he knows how I feel for him, even if he doesn't reciprocate those feelings.

Sam's gaze roams over my face, then he shakes his head and releases me before stepping closer and putting his hands to my waist in a gentle but firm way that makes my heart pound and my lower belly flutter.

'Wait. Please tell me again, Maz. Say it all again,' he says, his voice low and gravelly, his head bent so that only mere centimetres keep our lips apart.

My face burns hot and my entire body tingles under his intense gaze.

'So you can laugh at me?' I say, confused.

He chuckles low in his throat. 'No, you idiot.' He rests his warm forehead against mine, and his breath tickles my face. He smells sweet, like rum and cola. 'I would never laugh at you.' He draws back and stares into my eyes. 'You are my best friend... you are the most important person in my life and I think, no, I *know*...' He pauses and shakes his head.

'What? You know what?' I ask, my heart pounding furiously against my chest. I don't think my body can take this, Samuel holding me like this, our faces only inches apart. 'Tell me.'

'Okay, okay.' Sam licks his lips. 'Lately, the past year actually, I've felt like... you've been pulling away from me... being all weird... distant. I thought it meant you didn't care anymore. That you didn't like me, as a friend or as anything... I thought I was losing you.' He widens his eyes again and smiles, his breath warm against my cheek. 'That's why I find all of this... so hard to believe.' Samuel groans and pulls me closer to him. 'Because I've been in love with you for so long, Maz... but I thought you were rejecting me.'

Oh wow. Sam has this so wrong, and I've spent the past few years doing the same, assuming instead of outright asking.

'Wow. I've been pulling away because it's been so hard to be around you,' I say. 'Especially... you know, watching you with Angelica.'

'Geez, Maz, if only I knew. I would *never* have even dated Angelica.' He shakes his head again. 'Honestly, I thought I could never have you. That you'd never feel for me the same way I feel for you, the same way I've always felt for you.'

My heart flutters and my entire body comes to life as Samuel pulls me tight against him and wraps his arms around me.

'It's always been you, Maz. Always. Oh God... maybe things will be better. Maybe I won't feel so fucking sad anymore if I have you by my side.'

'Oh, Sam.' I reach up and stroke his face and he closes his eyes at my touch.

'Honestly, Maz, I haven't felt right for a long time,' he says, opening his eyes. 'Not just with things between you and me, but with myself. It's like... there's something wrong with me. Like my function setting is stuck on sadness.'

Something rustles behind the sand dunes in the bushes.

'Did you hear that?'

'Probably a quenda. There's heaps around here in the bush.' Samuel smiles down at me and strokes my face. 'Beautiful Maz.' His eyes shine with emotion. 'I can't believe it.'

I wrap my arms tighter around Sam's waist, revelling in the feeling of his warm body against mine. This is so surreal. I want to pinch myself in case I'm passed out somewhere back at the house. Maybe I refused to do the dare and was forced to drink that glass of bourbon Lizzie slid towards me and now I'm dreaming.

'You're not dreaming, dork,' Sam says, chuckling low in his throat.

'Please don't tell me I said all that out loud?'

Sam laughs, and the sound is like the magical tinkle of wind chimes in a warm summer breeze. I feel so light, so joyful, so euphoric. All the shame and guilt I've felt for harbouring feelings for my best friend have now vanished.

I lean forward to kiss him, but he jerks back.

'Wait. Sorry. I want... oh God... I want nothing more than to kiss you right now. But I have to tell Angelica first. Break it off with her. It's the right thing to do.'

'Yes,' I say, nodding and pulling away, my face flooding with heat. I want to bury myself beneath the dunes right now and never come back up, which is saying a lot because my greatest fear is being buried alive. 'Of course.'

'I know she's already got that Cameron guy but I want to start this' – he reaches for my hand and gives me a squeeze – 'to start *us*, the right way. There's so much I need to do... to sort my head out. I want to get better and I want to make myself a better person, grow into a better man for you.'

My heart soars as I squeeze his hand back.

'I'll help you in any way you need, even though I think you are perfect just the way you are.' I place my other hand over his, making a hand sandwich. 'We'll get through this together.'

Sam's eyes film over with tears and he blinks them away and laughs.

'Oh my God, Maz. This is freaking unbelievable.'

I release an embarrassingly shuddery and emotional breath. 'I can't believe we are really going to be together.'

Sam gazes down at me in a way that makes my heart skip a beat, then he smiles.

'You and me, Maz.'

'Always and forever,' I say.

Sam strokes my cheek with gentle fingers. 'Yep. Just like our favourite song.'

23

Now

'So you two did sneak around behind Angelica's back,' says Lizzie, blinking back tears. 'What a horrible thing for her to find out just before she died.'

'We don't know that she knew. We can only assume. But anyway, there wasn't any sneaking around. Samuel respected Angelica enough to want to tell her first, then break it off with her. We wouldn't have taken it any further until then.'

'Did he feel any guilt at all? At dumping Angelica for you?' Lizzie wipes the tears from her cheeks in swift, jerky motions.

'I guess he felt less guilty, we both did, because Angelica was already writing to that Cameron guy.'

Lizzie shakes her head and briefly raises her eyes to the ceiling. 'Don't make assumptions. You know nothing about Angelica and that guy, or why they were writing.'

I nod. 'That's true. And I'm sorry if I sound insensitive. Of course I felt bad… we both did. Because Angelica… she was so… she was such a beautiful soul. Neither of us wanted to hurt her.' I shiver and wrap myself up in a hug, my mind still there on the beach with Samuel.

'Well, she got hurt, didn't she? And it was either you or Samuel who did it.'

'Samuel would never do something like that!' Everybody turns to stare at Tamara, shocked by her outburst. 'He was too kind for that,' she continues, wiping a lone tear from her cheek.

'It's true. He was too kind to hurt anybody.' I shrug, recalling the excitement shining in his eyes. 'He honestly seemed so calm, so centred that night after we spoke. It was the first time I'd seen him so... so happy... in a long time.'

Lizzie shivers and rubs her arms, her eyes staring off into the distance.

'He must have killed himself, and Angelica must have found him. Maybe she was in such a state of shock at finding Samuel dead that she got dizzy and fell down the stairs...' Lizzie's voice trails off.

Tamara locks eyes with me before blinking rapidly and turning to Lizzie.

'Someone pushed her. I just know it. Nobody has ever fallen down those stairs. Ever. But that night Angelica did. Someone pushed her. Someone who had reason to want her gone.'

It's not lost on me that Tamara seems to be pinning the blame for Samuel's and Angelica's deaths on me. But after doing the same, blaming myself for the past ten years, I've finally realised the truth – that it wasn't my fault. Declaring my love for Samuel did not kill him. The photo Sienna took proves just how happy he looked, the happiest he'd been in years.

'It doesn't make sense to me, though.' I lock eyes with Lizzie. 'I'm not lying and I don't mean any disrespect to Angelica. But he was so happy. He couldn't wait for us to be together. He wouldn't have killed himself. There is no way. Something else must have happened.'

'But he told you he was depressed, and that he had been for a while. He may have reacted like that out of surprise when you told him about your feelings.' Lizzie wipes her eyes. 'But what if what you told him made things worse. What if he felt so awful for telling Angelica and he couldn't take the guilt and so he killed himself?'

A familiar ache returns to my heart, but I do my best to bury it.

'For a long time I believed that too, because I do remember him not being himself that day. He referenced wanting to end his life, kind of in a jokey but serious way, so many times.' I swallow down the tightness in my throat and blink away the stinging threat of tears. 'But, seeing this photo, it reminds me of how happy he was in that moment. It was like the thick fog of his depression was finally lifting. I don't think he would have killed himself at all.' I glance down at the photo. 'It's right here in front of us. Samuel was happy.'

Sienna wipes a tear from her cheek and gives me a sympathetic smile.

'I agree with you. He sounded happy too.' She reaches out and gives my hand a quick squeeze before glancing around the room and folding her arms across her chest. 'But I want everyone here to know that I never printed that photo. I haven't looked at it in over ten years. It's buried in my photo roll and to be honest, I don't know how anyone got a hold of it. I can't even imagine who here would do something like that.'

Tamara frowns and takes a step away from Lizzie.

'Oh come on, it wasn't me.' Lizzie looks at me, her eyes wide. 'How would I get access to her phone? I don't know her password and I'm not good with techie stuff.' She shakes her head. 'Seriously.'

'I have a good idea who could have done it,' says Lucas, meeting Sienna's eyes.

'Who?' Jake asks, his lone eye bright and alert with interest.

Lance gets up and slips an arm around my waist and I almost collapse against him in gratitude. I don't believe

I've ever needed Lance in my life as much as I need him right now.

Lucas mutters something beneath his breath to Sienna and storms out of the house, slamming the door behind him.

'What's his problem?' asks Tamara. She looks at us all. 'How about we search everyone's phone? The culprit probably still has the photo in their camera roll.'

'We don't have to do that,' Lizzie says, frowning.

'I'm going to talk to Lucas,' says Jake. 'See if I can convince him to come back inside. The sky's gonna open up again soon and he wouldn't want to be caught out in it.'

Sienna watches Jake leave the house and then glances at me, her eyes widening in alarm.

'I think I'd better go look for him too,' she says. 'He won't talk to anyone but me while he's upset.'

'I'll come with you,' I say, not wanting Sienna to head outside alone while Jake is lurking around the property. We know nothing about him other than the fact that he's dating Tamara.

Lance gives me a squeeze. 'How about you girls stay here where it's safe and I'll go and bring the boys in.'

I slip my arms around him and look up to meet his gaze, marvelling at the concern and the kindness in his eyes. I'm reminded of my last goodbye to Sam, and I shiver at the thought of never seeing Lance again. Because of this, I have a desperate urge to tell Lance that I love him, or to at least thank him for being a great boyfriend... for most of the time, if you ignore the cheating part.

'You need to let go of me, Maz,' he says, smiling gently, trying to loosen my hold on his waist.

'Oh, sorry,' I say, glancing at the others and blushing. 'Don't be too long. If you can't round them up in fifteen minutes, then come straight back.'

Thunder rumbles, closer this time, then lightening streaks through the room.

'Will do.' He looks up and smiles at Sienna kindly. 'Don't worry. We'll find him.'

'Jake too.' Tamara folds her arms across her chest, looking annoyed that nobody is concerned about her boyfriend. 'Just because he's got an eyepatch doesn't mean he's the villain.'

'Of course,' says Lance, giving her a nod. 'After I find the guys, we'll all be safe and sound under the same roof.'

'I hope so,' she says.

Lance leans down and whispers in my ear.

'Go upstairs. Wait for me and don't talk to anybody until I'm back.' He tucks a lock of my dark hair behind my ear. 'When I come back, we'll go to bed and watch the storm roll in... and talk all night if you like. Just you and me.'

Lance's words remind me so much of Samuel's last words to me, and my heart flutters in panic. I wrap my arms around his neck and pull him down towards me, then kiss him passionately until my lips begin to sting. I don't care that everyone is watching.

'This is beyond inappropriate,' says Lizzie. I can practically hear her eyeroll.

Nobody else says a word.

'See you soon.' Lance looks at me, long and deep, like he wants to study my face and commit it to memory. I do the same with him. Then I watch him walk out the door and try to ignore the fact that I'm feeling déjà vu.

'Who needs another shot?' asks Lizzie, sounding tired. She taps the small shot glass against the tabletop.

'I'm heading upstairs,' I say, not bothering to wait to hear what the others say about me or my confession. I simply don't care what they think anymore and I'm not sure whom to trust after knowing someone planted that photo especially for my discomfort. Tamara hinting at my involvement in Angelica's death hurts too. I'm just going to stay away from everyone until Lance comes back.

I glance at my phone. In fifteen minutes Lance will return, that is, if he keeps his promise. I just have to wait upstairs in the bedroom until he comes. I'll lock the door until then.

As I take the candlelit stairs, a shadow passes across the top floor. Maybe it's Will. Great. The last thing I need now is another sexual proposition. Not while all this drama is going on.

But when I get to the top of the stairs, Will is nowhere to be found. Maybe the shadow was caused by a flicker of lightning. There's no light beneath the master bedroom so maybe Will's asleep already.

I enter my bedroom, grateful to shut the door behind me, but when I look up and see a man sitting on the edge of the bed, I freeze.

'What are you doing here?'

24

'I'll scream if you don't get out in three seconds. One... Two...'

'Wait. Don't scream. I'm not here to proposition you.' Will raises two palms and grimaces, having the decency to blush. 'I've got clothes on, see?'

'Get to the point.' My face is too rigid to crack a smile at his pathetic attempt at humour.

Will stands up and I take a step closer to the door.

'Okay, I understand why you're reacting like this. I fully get it. But I'm here to let you know, to warn you, to watch your back.'

I fold my arms across my chest and sigh. It's pretty obvious I need to watch my back after someone planted that photograph in my room.

'Is it Lizzie? Do you know something that I don't?'

Will shifts his gaze to the floor and rubs his chin. 'I can't say. But I just felt I needed to warn you. Stay here, in your room, until the rain clears up tomorrow and just leave. I wouldn't trust anyone if I were you.'

'Everything you're saying is valid, but... why should I trust what you say? You're the guy who tried to sleep with me only a few hours ago, the same guy who is dating my friend.'

He raises his brows and scratches the back of his neck. 'I'd hardly call you friends. Lizzie hasn't exactly been treating you the way a friend should... neither have the others. It's screwed up. But it might not be Lizzie's fault.'

'What do you mean?'

Will meets my gaze and rubs his chin. 'I think she may have… mixed up her meds or maybe brought the wrong ones with her. To be honest, I didn't know she was on antidepressants. She told me she was recovering from a brain tumour when I first met her. Said she's on pain meds.' He nods towards the door and clears his throat. 'I've said too much already, and it's none of my business so I probably shouldn't have told you all that.'

I step out of the way, wondering what this means. Lizzie never mentioned anything about a brain tumour, but it would explain the scar running along her scalp. Poor Lizzie.

'Thanks for letting me know. I won't say anything to Lizzie about it.'

He nods. 'Just try to stay out of trouble… it's difficult to explain but, I've got a feeling that something bad is going to happen.' He shivers, as though a sudden gust of icy wind has blown through him, and reaches for the doorknob. 'I should have asked for more information from Lizzie before saying yes. Some kind of background…' His voice trails off and he shakes his head, his face grave and as bleak and troubled as the weather thrashing against the bedroom window. 'I just wish I never came to this place, to be honest.'

As he leaves the room, I swear I hear him muttering something about hoping that his dad is okay. Why wouldn't his dad be okay, wherever he is? And what does his dad have to do with any of this?

'Wait, Will,' I whisper through a gap in the open door. 'Is everything okay? I mean, with you?'

He turns to face me, his dark eyes glimmering in the candlelight, seemingly full of regret.

'No. Nothing is okay. I'm just… ashamed. Ashamed of what I've done. Of what I agreed to do. It's not who I am.'

'What are you talking about?'

'Goodnight, Marilyn.'

I watch him disappear into the opposite bedroom, my heart racing.

Part of me wants to run downstairs and demand that Lizzie tells me what's going on with Will, but the other half of me doesn't want to leave this room because of Will's dire warning. Strangely enough, although I don't know the man, I somehow feel as though I can trust him. He feels shame and regret, perhaps for propositioning me in the bathroom, which means that he at least has a conscience. Then there's Lizzie recovering from brain surgery. How awful. I wish I'd kept in touch. I could have been there for her and supported her through it.

I collapse onto the super soft bed and try not to succumb to the instant exhaustion that overcomes me while I check my phone for the time. Lance will be back soon, and then the two of us can stay up all night talking into the early hours. As soon as dawn arrives, we'll drive up to the track and wait beside it until it dries up, then we'll finally leave this place behind.

Just as a dazzling flash of lightning illuminates the sky and the beach below, I glance out the window.

Wait… what was that?

Or, more importantly, *who* was that?

I slide off the bed, my heart hammering against my chest, and rush to stand at the window, praying for another flash in the sky.

Someone was running. Could it have been Lucas?

It's pitch black out there, so after the next roll of thunder I wait, my breath held while I count, my eyes searching the darkness.

In a flash the beach is brilliantly lit once more, but this time it is empty, only the churning sea foaming at the silvery shore.

Could it have been my imagination?

I wait again for more lightning, and when it finally comes, my stomach churns at what I see.

Footprints in the sand.

Not just one set.

Whoever it was running on the beach, someone was chasing him.

Could Jake or Lance have simply been trying to coax Lucas back to the safety of the house? Could it be as innocent as that?

Rain begins to fall, hard and heavy, and my pulse quickens when I look at my phone. Lance should have returned by now. But then again if that was Lucas I saw running, it may take a lot longer than fifteen minutes for Lance to convince him to come back.

When the sky lights up again, the footsteps are gone, washed away by the rain, as though it never happened.

The evidence is gone.

I shake my head and tell myself to shut up.

Just because something bad occurred the last time I was here, doesn't mean that anything terrible is set to happen this weekend. This holiday house isn't cursed and the spirits of our dead friends aren't hell-bent on revenge like Sienna suggested earlier.

Still, I slip into bed and slide down low beneath the covers. While the storm rages outside, I play music on my phone to pass the time. Lance's favourite artist. It cheers me up a little. Lance will be here soon. He'll tell me stories to make me laugh and reassure me that everything is going to turn out okay. Then we'll leave tomorrow as soon as the track dries up.

Everything is going to be okay.

Sometime later, I open my eyes and sit up in bed with a start, my head pounding and my mouth dry. I squint my eyes at the fading light of the candle which has all but melted into a puddle of clear wax and see that Lance's side of the bed hasn't been touched.

Oh God, I must have fallen asleep, hopefully for only a few minutes. But when I finally locate my phone deep beneath the covers, I see the time and my heart constricts in panic.

It's 2am. Two hours since Lance said he'd be back in fifteen minutes.

I get up out of bed and leave the room.

The entire house is quiet as I peer down the stairs, the only sound is the wind whistling through the cracks from outside. My heart stutters on its beat.

Something is wrong.

Something is very wrong.

I head downstairs, my heart hammering against my chest.

But the first step creaks beneath my bare foot and only a few seconds later the master bedroom door opens and a dark shadow appears.

'Don't go down there,' Will whispers harshly, stepping into view.

'Why? I need to find Lance.'

He sighs and runs his hands down his face, muttering something I can't quite hear.

Then he looks at me. 'Don't say I didn't warn you.'

25

Downstairs, I find Sienna and Tamara in the kitchen, hugging by the breakfast bar where stained wine glasses and stacked dirty plates litter the marble benchtop. In the dying light of a melted candle, Sienna's tears glisten against her cheeks, a sight that tightens my chest.

I clasp my hands together and clear my throat. 'Has something happened?'

The girls don't respond, but Tamara throws me a loaded look. Loaded with what? I can't even begin to guess.

'Please tell me the boys came back and… I don't know, got drunk and passed out in the living room. Just tell me they're safe.'

Sienna pulls away from Tamara and hastily rubs the dampness from her cheeks with her pyjama shirtsleeve.

'Lucas,' she croaks and then draws a shaky breath. 'Lucas didn't come back.'

'Neither did Lance,' I say.

Outside, the rain has eased and is now tapping lightly against the tin roof, drumming a steadier rhythm than my heart.

'I'm worried, Maz,' Sienna says, wringing her hands together. 'Lucas hates the rain and getting wet. He wouldn't stay out there… unless something bad happened to him.'

'Maybe they took shelter somewhere else?' I suggest hopefully to Sienna, then look at Tamara. 'Did Jake return?'

'Yeah. He's asleep. Lance came back as well.' She folds her arms across her ample chest and pointedly avoids my gaze.

'What? They both came back without Lucas?'

My head throbs with a sudden headache. So where is Lance if he didn't join me in the bedroom?

'What happened?' I ask Tamara, who continues to avoid my gaze. 'Why are you being weird?'

When she doesn't answer me I turn to Sienna who shrugs and also looks away.

Tamara glances across to the dim, candlelit entrance of the living room and I follow her gaze to where I can barely make out a blob of wet clothes on the floor. My stomach churns. I'm not sure what that pile of clothes means, but I'm going to find out.

I take a candle from the counter, which has melted down to a crater-like mass of hot wax on the saucer it rests on, but still burns enough to light my way. As I get closer I can confirm that the clothes belong to Lance. He was wearing a dark blue shirt and there is a dark blue shirt, sopping wet and discarded on top of the pile.

'I bet he kept drinking and flaked,' I mutter beneath my breath, mildly annoyed that he didn't come up to my room like he promised. I had been worried sick the entire time. Well, asleep and worried sick, but copious amounts of red wine makes you sleepy.

Sienna appears at my side, tugging on my shirtsleeve. 'Maybe you don't want to see this.'

'No. She needs to see it,' Tamara says. 'She needs to–'

'What the...' I say, cutting her off as the warm glow of candlelight illuminates enough of the living room for me to see Lance and Lizzie entwined on the couch. 'Seriously?'

Lizzie stirs. Tamara and Sienna close rank behind me.

'Hey.' Lizzie blinks several times and then puts a hand to her mouth, miming shock. 'Oh... looks like I spent some time with your boyfriend behind your back.' She gets up, wearing only a singlet and her underwear, looking painfully skinny.

Will's warning comes to mind, along with what he told me about Lizzie's meds.

'Lance is actually not my boyfriend.'

My words wipe the grin from Lizzie's face. She takes a couple of steps forward, the dark circles beneath her eyes appearing deeper in the yellowy glow of the candle's flame.

'What do you mean?'

I drop my shoulders and release a sigh. 'Lance is a serial cheater. We broke up a last month. He only came on this trip because my car broke down this morning and I needed someone to drive me.'

Lizzie looks from me and back to Lance who is now only just beginning to stir. He's always been a solid sleeper and takes ages to wake, even in the middle of a drama like this.

'Are you telling the truth?'

'What does it matter? You obviously thought it was okay to sleep with him, even though you believed he was my boyfriend at the time.'

'Hurts, doesn't it?' Lizzie watches my face closely for a reaction.

'Well, we're not together anymore and I've been hurt too many times in the past for this to bother me now.'

The candle spits a tiny spray of sparks from its liquid grave before it dies, leaving us all standing in the dark, with only the dim glow of the starlit beach through the living room window.

I meet Lizzie's shiny eyes with my own. 'Okay, it does hurt a bit. Because you're my friend.' I shrug, unsure what to say. How odd that Will, her boyfriend, propositioned *me* only a few hours ago. Maybe they have one of those open relationships.

'Well, you know all about that, don't you, Maz?' she says, her voice emotional and tight as she pushes past me and heads upstairs, her feet barely touching each step as she disappears up and onto the second floor.

'She set me up,' says Lance, who is finally awake and has the decency to wrap a crocheted blanket around his naked body after he sits up. 'I didn't do anything. I swear. She made me strip in the laundry because I was soaked. Then...' He pauses to scratch his head. 'Then she led me here... to this couch. I fell asleep. I swear to you, Maz, I did nothing. I mean, I don't think I did.' He frowns.

I fold my arms across my chest and shake my head because I have no words.

'But if I did do anything, then it's because she took advantage.'

He blinks and even though it's dark, I swear I can see remorse shining in his eyes. It almost makes me feel sorry for him. Almost.

'Poor you,' I say, shrugging away Sienna and Tamara's well-meaning hands from my shoulders. I'm not a victim. I'm just annoyed. Maybe humiliated a little. But getting hurt by Lance is something to be expected now. I can't pretend to be shocked because I'm not.

'That's not fair and you know it.' He gets up and points a finger in my face. 'You have a problem, Maz. You're always waiting around for me to slip up. It's almost as though you want me to.' The last sentence comes out softly, almost a whisper, and Lance drops his head into his hands, the crocheted blanket dropping to the floor.

Sienna and Tamara gasp in unison at Lance's nakedness and quietly leave the room.

'Oh shit, I'm sorry, Maz. I'm being a dickhead. I think the booze and... and this place and your screwed-up friends... everything has got me all rattled.'

He stumbles over to the wet pile of clothes and scoops everything up into his arms and heads upstairs, his naked butt the last I see of him before he slams the bedroom door shut.

Well, there's no way I'll be returning to the bedroom. I'm wide awake anyway and I'm determined that the next place I lay my head will be my own pillow at home.

I close my eyes and picture my house, the place I grew up in which was gifted to me by my late mother. A hot shower and a mug of sweet milky tea, then my own comfy bed. I'll have to get my car booked into the garage to get fixed and pack up Lance's belongings so that his exit from my life is swift and not drawn out in a way that might make me soften and allow him to stay any longer than necessary. But I can handle all of that. I just need to get home first.

The wind grows wilder outside, as though in response to my thoughts, sounding strong enough to carry me away... or keep me here. Maybe I should go and stand on the beach and let it take me? It may be my only way out.

I shake my head free of such crazy thoughts and return to the kitchen where the girls are making themselves a hot drink, the kettle boiling noisily. It's a comforting sound, reminding me that the world carries on. That even if you do find your boyfriend – or your ex-boyfriend – naked on the couch with one of your old friends, it's not the end of the world. The sun will still set and rise, tea can be brewed. Life can go on.

'I might go for a walk,' I say to the girls. There's a fire in my belly now. I'm ready to take charge of my life, get it back on track. Maybe I'll find a stick on the beach and carve a fresh list of future goals I want to achieve into the sand. Let the choppy sea wash it away and send my dreams out to the universe.

'Is that wise?' Tamara nods towards Sienna. 'Lucas is still missing, remember? I don't think anyone should leave this house until morning.'

'I need to get out. I need air. And who knows, I might find him.' I drum the countertop with my fingers. 'Did the guys say which direction Lucas headed?' As soon as the words leave my lips, I remember, with a shiver, what I saw last night through the window. Or at least, what I think I saw.

Sienna watches me closely and turns pale, as though she can read my mind.

'The boys told Tamara that they think he tried to hike through the bush to get to the main road. He wanted to get help so we can all leave here first thing in the morning. But because there's no phone signal I have no way of contacting him.'

'But surely he would have come back and told you if he was planning on trekking out so far.'

'That's what I said. He'd want me with him.'

'Jake tried to stop him.' Tamara takes a jar of sugar out of the pantry and sets it on the counter by the steaming kettle. 'He said that Lucas seemed pretty determined and didn't want you to worry. That's probably why he didn't come and tell you, because you probably wouldn't have let him go.'

Sienna's dark eyes well with tears. 'Oh God. That sounds like Lucas. He's always putting my wellbeing first. I just hope he's okay.'

Lucas running keeps flashing through my mind, but I try to appear as neutral as possible, for Sienna's benefit.

'Well, I can't sleep so I'm going to go out for a walk anyway. It can't hurt for me to have a look around.'

Sienna nods and looks calmer already. There may even be a sparkle of hope in her eyes.

'I'll come. In case Lucas has gotten into some kind of trouble and needs me.'

'Okay.' I smile at Sienna, glad to have her company. 'Let's go.'

26

Tamara hovers by the door as we put our shoes on. 'I'll stay here in case he comes back while you're out.'

'God, I hope he does.' Sienna closes her eyes when she says it, as though in prayer.

'I'm sure he'll be okay,' Tamara says, reaching out to touch Sienna's arm. She also grabs my hand and gives it a squeeze. 'Be safe. Don't stay out there too long, or go too far, please. The boys said there are patches of quicksand in the bushland due to the storm. I don't want either of you sucked away underground so stay away from the bush.'

I shudder. My biggest fear is being buried alive. I developed the fear after I watched a film where the main character was thrown into a hole and covered over with sand and given only a straw with which to breathe. I was only five years of age. My mum thought I'd gone to bed while she watched the movie, but I sat in my pyjamas in the hallway, peeping around the wall as I always did on Sunday nights.

Tamara gives my hand another squeeze. 'Sorry. I don't mean to scare you. I just want you both to stay safe. Stick to the beach, the open, clear places...'

'We will. We'll just take a quick look around the house and on the beach in case he's lost or sheltering somewhere, like at Lizzie's dad's workshop.' I remember Lizzie showing us her dad's special place, an old shed that sits further along the beach away from the house, along the fringe of the bushland. He used to create beach art there, with driftwood and shells.

I catch the look of horror on Tamara's face and raise my palms. 'It's not too deep in the bush, you can see it from the beach, so I doubt there'll be quicksand there. Lucas may have taken shelter there so it's worth a look.'

'Oh,' Tamara says, frowning. 'Lizzie said the shed was taken down after her dad passed away. Apparently it needed repairing but after he died her mum thought it best to tear it down. You know, for safety reasons. I think white ants had completely destroyed most of it anyway, so there's no shed anymore.'

The shed used to stand in the direction the figure was running in when I saw him on the beach through the upstairs window. I was half hoping to open the shed door to find Lucas huddled in there sheltering from this weather. But now there's no chance of that.

Something is not right here. If the figure I saw was Lucas, and he truly left to find the road, as Tamara said, then why would he have run across the beach like that in the opposite direction? Surely he would have followed the track to the main highway.

'Okay, well if the shed's gone, then maybe we can check the basement,' I say, 'and do a quick circle around the property, just to be sure.'

'Good idea,' says Sienna, who looks like she's knows something that I don't. 'But let's check the beach first.'

'I don't like this,' says Tamara, wringing her hands. 'I think you two should stay in the house where it's safe.'

'We'll be okay.' I offer her a reassuring smile. 'A quick walk along the beach and around the outside of the house and then we'll come right back.'

'Don't be long, please. I care about you both so much. I've been so lonely these past ten years.' Something glistens against Tamara's cheeks and I realise that she's crying. 'And it's been so good to see you guys again.'

'Oh, Tams,' I say. I wish I could say more, but truth be told, I feel the same. I've wanted so much, over the past ten years, to contact them all, to rekindle our old friendships. But I've been too frightened to reach out for fear of rejection.

'Lizzie is great...' Tamara sniffs and wipes her cheeks. 'But she's not like you two. She's changed. It's actually been hard work, being her friend, supporting her.'

I stare at Tamara, confused.

'Wait. Have you been seeing Lizzie this whole time?'

Tamara looks from Sienna to me and nods. 'Sorry. She told me not to say anything.'

When I glance at Sienna, she shrugs. 'I've been seeing Lizzie too – only recently... we met for the first time only a couple of months ago.'

They both look at me expectantly and I shake my head as I try to look as unhurt as possible.

'No. I hadn't heard from Lizzie until she sent me the invitation for this weekend.'

It all makes sense now. The weirdness of Lizzie this weekend, how she keeps flirting and messing around with Lance, and aiming seemingly harmless but sharp little barbs at me. I guess I've been trying to deny what's been clear since the moment I arrived. That Lizzie blames me for what happened here ten years ago.

'Be careful around Lizzie,' warns Tamara. 'She isn't exactly the same girl we knew and loved ten years ago. She's... she's kind of stuck in the past.' Tamara releases a noisy sigh, as though relieved to be finally freeing herself of this heavy burden.

'Poor Lizzie,' I say, thinking about what Will told me about Lizzie's brain tumour. I'm not sure that the others know about it so I stay silent. But seeing as they've all been keeping in touch, they probably know already.

'When she gets really bad, at her absolute worst, she starts replaying the events of that night, over and over again. I think it traumatised her deeply.' Tamara blinks, her eyes glimmering with unshed tears. 'But I just wish she could move forward from it all, you know? I hate being reminded of everything that happened.' Her hands become fists and anger flares in her cheeks.

Sienna reaches out to touch Tamara but she flinches and Sienna retracts her hand.

'Sorry. I'm just... all emotional.' Tamara wipes her face again and sighs. 'Anyway, just tread carefully around her, please. She spent a bit of time in a mental health facility after her dad died. Her mum put her in there after Lizzie shaved her head and started cutting herself. But I think her time there made her worse, to be honest. It made her start to obsess about what happened. She had too much time to think while she was locked away and now... it's become a sort of... obsession.'

Sienna shakes her head. 'I feel so bad for Lizzie... but right now we need to find Lucas. He's out there somewhere, all alone...' Her voice breaks. 'All alone. I just know he wouldn't have left me without telling me first.'

'Let's go.' I give Tamara a quick hug and take a step back. 'We'll be okay. I promise.'

Sienna swings the front door wide open and a huge gust of wind nearly blows us off our feet.

The coat rack topples over again, sending hats, scarfs and umbrellas flying down the hallway.

'Quick,' I say, and shove Sienna out the door and into the blackness of the night, leaving Tamara to tidy up the mess we left behind.

Once we leave the porch and our shoes hit the sand, Sienna breathes a sigh of relief.

'Thank God,' she says, having to almost shout over the wind, her red hair whipping her face. 'I just needed to get away from her. Even if it means being out here in this crazy weather.'

I smile and say nothing. I'm just grateful to be breathing in fresh air, even if it means putting up with these strong winds. All that scented candle wax was giving me a headache.

Sienna sweeps her hair out of her face and throws me a look. 'I feel bad for saying this, Maz, but I don't trust Tamara. There's something off about her, and Lucas told me that he doesn't trust Jake either. He caught him trying to pocket my phone after I put it on charge in the kitchen.'

'Really? What happened? How did he explain himself?'

'When Lucas accused him, Jake pretended he'd grabbed the wrong phone by mistake.' Sienna shrugs. 'He does happen to have the same phone as me. Same colour too. But if Lucas doesn't trust him, then neither do I.'

Goosebumps prickle my skin, from the wind or Sienna's talk of her suspicions, I can't be sure.

'Let's just concentrate on finding Lucas,' I say. 'I bet he's already reached the main road and is probably in a hotel, sipping on hot chocolate while he calls emergency services and lets them know we're stranded here.'

'But it would take hours to get to the main road,' says Sienna.

'I know. But it's a nice thought.'

Sienna smiles.

We link arms and brace ourselves against the onslaught of the wind as we trudge our way through the wet sand away from the house and towards the beach.

Once we're over the dunes, the beach opens up and stretches endlessly beneath a black, star-dotted sky. The dark sea churns and froths at our feet, soaking into our shoes as I lead Sienna in the direction I last saw Lucas.

'Lucas,' she calls out every minute or so. I do the same. But after walking the beach for at least half an hour, our voices hoarse, I suggest we turn back.

Drops of rain start to pelt down upon us.

'Come on, Sienna. If he was out here he would have answered our calls. Let's go back.'

Sienna grabs my arm and digs her nail into my flesh through my shirt.

'No. We keep searching.' She clenches her jaw, her gritted teeth glowing beneath the light of the stars. 'How can you even think of giving up?'

The hairs on the back of my neck prickle. Being out here on a deserted beach with a friend who has grown into somebody that I don't recognise, leaves me feeling uneasy. I'm starting to wish we'd listened to Tamara and stayed at the house.

'Of course. I don't mean give up,' I say, 'I mean we should head back to check around the outside of the house and the basement. We haven't looked there yet.'

'I guess so. Let's go then.'

Sienna tightens her grip on my arm as she drags me back towards the house. I try to loosen her hold but she grips me even tighter, which is surprising given how tiny she is compared to me.

'Sienna. Let me go, will you?'

Sienna stops in her tracks and glances at my arm and immediately lets me go, her hands rising up to her face. 'Oh my God, I'm so sorry, Maz. I hope I didn't hurt you.'

'It's all good.' I rub at the place where her nails had dug in. 'But bloody hell, you must go to the gym or something. That's one tight grip.'

'Sorry. I'm just worried.' Sienna stares at me, her face deathly serious. 'If something has happened to Lucas... I just don't know what I'll do, Maz.'

27

Then

The moon is working its magic tonight, casting a silver lining on everything it touches. I plonk myself down on the cool sand and watch the dark, glittering water gently lap the shore as I wait for Samuel, my anticipation growing as each minute passes.

My stomach is in knots as I alternate between fear and joy. How will Angelica take the news that her boyfriend is in love with another, that other person being one of her friends? Will she be okay with it because she already has this thing with that Cameron guy? Relieved because she was looking for a way out anyway? Or will she feel betrayed that her boyfriend and her friend have kept their true feelings from her?

I wonder if she'll accuse me of stealing Samuel away from her. Not that I have or could ever steal Samuel from anyone. He's not a possession. This is his own choice.

Then there's Tamara too. Will she also feel betrayed by me? Although she's never said it out loud, it's been clear to me for a long while that she has feelings for Samuel. I'm going to have to apologise for not telling her the truth earlier.

A seagull flaps overhead, against the star-studded black sky. I watch it as it hovers and studies me for a moment, before it deems me safe, or perhaps too boring, then gently soars over the sea and lands somewhere in the distance, a small silvery shape bobbing along the surface.

Unable to sit around waiting any longer, I get up and dust the sand from my denim shorts and walk along the shore, the cool foamy water tickling my ankles.

I wish Samuel would get back here already so that we can enjoy a nice long walk together and make plans for our future. Of course, once we've had some time to ourselves, alone, to discuss things, I'm hoping that we can return to the house and still be welcomed by everyone. I'd hate us to become ostracized from the group because of our feelings for each other. We still have an entire week of our leavers' holiday to enjoy.

After around twenty minutes or so, that lone seagull has flapped its wings and flown away and I'm pacing the sandy shore, alone and impatient.

Then out of nowhere, I hear raised voices, ever so faintly, coming from the house and I stop pacing. Over the rampant thud of my pulse, I strain my ears to listen. It's a guy... Samuel or Brayden, raising their voice. I've never heard Samuel raise his voice, ever, in the entire time I've known him which is since kindergarten. Of course, it could be Brayden. Sienna is always telling him off about one thing or another and they're always at each other, in a playful kind of way. But I know I'm grasping at straws. This guy sounds distressed. It's got to be Samuel.

But despite what he'd set out to do, I can't imagine him raising his voice to Angelica, no matter how badly she reacts to what he's telling her.

Something must be seriously wrong.

My stomach churns as I weigh up what to do. Showing up and intervening could make things worse. What girl wants to see her ex-boyfriend's new girlfriend during or right after they've broken up? But I can't stand out here on the beach all night. I've got to go face up to the mess Sam and I have created.

The light in the living room is still on. Perhaps Brayden stripped down to nothing during poker and Sienna yelled at him to put his clothes back on. Maybe all the carrying on was him refusing. I nod and allow myself to believe the possibility, so I don't have to entertain the idea that Samuel is upset and in distress.

The upstairs light is also on so I can only assume that Samuel is still up there speaking, or arguing, with Angelica.

Hurry up, Sam.

I climb the dunes with slow steps, my bare feet plunging deep into the fine sand, my stomach swirling. Although I don't want to go back to the house, I need to do this. I need to face up to what I've done. The chaos I've created by telling Samuel that I'm in love with him. I'm probably going to be forever remembered by my friends as the one who ruined leavers' week. But if it means getting to be with Samuel, then I can handle it. With Samuel by my side, I'll be able to handle anything life throws at me from now on.

Back at the house a door slams, the sound echoing across the dunes towards me. I slow my step.

Oh God. It's been done.

Will I cross paths with Samuel or Angelica? Will Angelica hate me? Will Samuel see me and have regrets? Was it just the alcohol talking when he confessed his love for me? He did seem pretty tipsy.

But it's not Angelica or Samuel whom I see charging down the path toward the beach, it's Tamara.

'Tamara!'

My friend doesn't flinch, she doesn't even look up. She must be super distracted... or perhaps upset. Maybe she knows. She may have overhead Samuel telling Angelica.

Oh no.

I call her name again and catch up to her, reaching for her arm and she gasps, as though surprised to see me, and stops running.

'What's wrong? Did something happen?'

Tamara shrugs herself out of my touch and wipes the tears from her face with the palms of her shaking hands.

'You wouldn't understand, *Maz*, okay? You just wouldn't.'

Fear flutters around in my ribcage. The way she said my name... she must know. Oh God. My heart breaks for her. Tamara and I have always been so close. Why on earth didn't I think things through? I should have told Tamara first, before she heard it from anyone else, instead of hiding out on the beach like a criminal.

I watch as more tears flood my friend's cheeks and my throat thickens. If I'd have known her feelings for Samuel were this strong I would have probably waited until after leavers' week to confess my feelings to him. I open my arms and Tamara surprisingly allows me to wrap them around her.

'Why can't he love me?' She sobs into my shoulder.

As she trembles against me, I feel something firm pressing into my chest and realise that Tamara is wearing her chicken fillets, the jelly bra fillers she uses to make her breasts appear fuller. She normally only wears them to parties or on a night out. Then I notice that she's wearing a red dress, and that her tears have smeared freshly applied makeup. Makeup that she wasn't wearing earlier.

Oh God. Tamara must have dressed up for Samuel. Maybe she chose tonight, of all nights, to make her own declaration.

'I hate him. I hate him. I hate him.'

I can't help but stiffen at her words, at the malice towards Samuel, but I keep calm as I pull away and look Tamara in the eye.

'What happened, Tams?'

'Sam... he told me he's in love. He told me that he's never looked at me in that way, that he'll never look at me in the romantic way... and that he's in love.'

'With whom?' I ask, feeling like a coward. I shouldn't be making her say it out loud. I should be telling her myself.

Tamara looks at me, her eyes red.

'With Angelica... who else? Shouldn't you know this? You're his best friend.' Her eyes narrow, reducing them to dark slits.

'He loves *Angelica*?' I ask, dumbfounded. 'He told you this just now?'

Tamara wipes her face and frowns and I swear there is something glittering in her eyes, something that tells me that she is enjoying this. Maybe she knows about my feelings. Maybe Samuel told her.

But why, when he told me he loved me only half an hour ago, would he confess to loving Angelica? Why didn't he tell Tamara that he loved *me*?

Maybe he made a mistake... I mean, he is drunk. He could have switched our names accidentally. That's got to be it.

'He loves Angelica,' she says, and this time, I definitely see the malice glittering in her eyes. 'He will only ever love her.'

'That's not true,' I whisper.

'It is.' Tamara's eyes glitter with fresh tears but she blinks them away.

28

Now

Dim candlelight glows weakly from the windows of the house as we struggle over the wet dunes. I shiver, not just from being tossed about by the brutal wind, but also at the image of Lucas running along the beach that keeps haunting me.

Lucas running and someone giving chase, then the tell-tale footsteps.

When we reach the path which leads to the house, I slow my steps. 'Wait. Sienna. I need to tell you something.'

She stops but doesn't turn around. I can tell she's desperate to keep moving.

'Please, don't tell me anything bad.' She begins pacing back and forth, hands on her slim hips, while trying to catch her breath in this howling wind. When she finally looks at me, the whites of her eyes are glowing. 'Actually, no. Just spit it out.'

I nod, my heart racing.

'I saw him... Lucas... earlier. At least I think I did. I was upstairs and when lightning flashed, I thought I saw him running along this beach.'

Sienna looks at me for a long time, her mouth open. 'Why didn't you tell me?' She covers her mouth with her hands. 'Oh my God. Which direction was he running in?'

I nod south. 'Where Lizzie's dad's workshop used to be. I should have told you, I'm so sorry. He was with someone, so I thought... I thought Lance or Jake were trying to convince him to come back. I thought they'd all return together.'

Sienna opens her mouth to say something, but then closes it and shakes her head before she storms off, back in the direction of the beach.

'Where are you going?'

'To Lizzie's dad's shed. *Alone*.'

'But Tamara said there is no shed,' I say, following Sienna over the dunes. Salty air whips my hair and a fine mist of sand across my face.

'Yeah, well, I don't believe her. I didn't want to say it in front of her, but Lucas and I took a walk earlier today, while it was still light, and I thought I saw the dark shape of the shed peeking through the bushes. I was going to show Lucas some of Lizzie's dad's artwork, but then the rain started and we ran back to the house. But I swear I saw it.'

'Oh, well, I guess that's a good thing.' Hope swells in my chest, despite the nagging feeling that something is off here, because, why on earth would Tamara lie about the workshop being torn down? Was she simply trying to deter us from leaving the house?

'The rain was falling so hard earlier, I bet Lucas is taking shelter,' I say.

'Let's hope.' Sienna increases her pace as she starts to run along the beach. 'But the fact that Tamara lied about it worries me,' she shouts over the wind. 'Why would she do that?'

'She wanted us to stay. Maybe she lied to keep us at the house for our own safety, who knows?'

'Yeah well, I'm sick of everyone lying. I don't know who to believe anymore.'

A harsh sound, the grind of a metal hinge, loud enough to cut through the howl of the wind, screeches through the night.

Sienna stops in her tracks and puts a hand to my arm.

'What was that?'

My pulse thunders in my ears, there's no mistaking that sound. It's the same sound that is forever etched in my memory. It's the very sound I heard moments before I found Samuel and Angelica.

'It's the metal hatch of the basement.'

'Lucas!' Sienna takes off in the direction of the house.

I follow, running faster than I've ever done in my life.

As we near the house, I run ahead of Sienna so that I can warn her to keep quiet. She nods and we slow down, then with our palms brushing lightly against the rendered wall, we tiptoe around the bend, where even in the dark of the night, we can see that the basement hatch is open like a gaping mouth.

I strain my ears for anything, voices, a sound, but can't hear anything but the howling wind.

'I'm going in,' Sienna whispers. 'If Lucas is down there...'

I reach out and lightly squeeze her hand.

'I know. But we need to be careful. We don't know who or what's in there.' I lower my voice. 'Let's take it slow and try not to make a sound.'

Sienna ignores my pleas and seizes my hand, dragging me towards the open hatch, but she stifles a scream when a head emerges out of the hole.

'Jake?' I whisper, once I see the dark patch. 'What are you doing down in the basement so late?'

Sienna gets out her phone and uses it as a torch.

Jake shields the light from his face with a single hand and growls.

'Get that effing thing out of my face.'

My heart flutters in panic when I see that his black eyepatch is slightly askew.

'What?' Jake regards me with two perfect blue eyes and I can't help but gasp. I'd just assumed, when I first met him, that he wore the patch because he'd lost an eye at some stage of his life.

'Your patch, it's...' My voice trails off as Jake readjusts his eyepatch so that only a single eye blinks back at me.

'Happy now?'

'We're looking for Lucas.'

'Yeah, well, there's nothing down there.' Jake rubs the back of his neck and yawns.

'What were you doing down there?' I ask, immediately suspicious, the hairs on the back of my neck prickling. 'Tamara said you'd gone to sleep.'

'Tams woke me up. She was worried something had happened to you two and told me to check the basement in case.'

'In case what?' Sienna asks, gripping my hand tighter still. 'You're lying. I bet Lucas is down there.' She leans towards the hole. 'Lucas!'

'There's nobody down there. Look.' Jake turns on the torch feature of his own phone and holds it above the dark trapdoor hatch. 'There's no one there.'

'I want to go see for myself,' says Sienna.

Jake shakes his head at Sienna and then looks at me. 'Trust me. There's nobody down there. Here.' He hands me his phone. 'Go look for yourself.'

I take the phone and shine its light down the hatch, illuminating the staircase right down to the basement floor. No blood, thank God. But my heart still races as I take the first step, then the second, taking my time because the wind keeps whipping my hair across my eyes. At the sixth step, halfway down, I pause. The basement is so quiet and still and the air in here feels warm without the wind attacking me.

'Lucas?'

Silence. I shine Jake's phone around the basement, moving the light extra quickly past the place where Samuel took his last breath. The windchimes that hang suspended from the ceiling there, tinkle. Maybe the spirit of Samuel knows I'm here, or he could be trying to tell me something.

But it's a foolish, wishful thought, because Samuel's long gone. And this basement is empty.

'There's no one here,' I say, feeling both relieved and also sad. Because it means that Lucas is still missing. 'Jake's telling the truth.'

When I try to turn so that I can climb back up the stairs, Sienna blocks my way.

'No. Go further down. Check it out properly.' Sienna grips my arm and leans into me.

Feeling claustrophobic, and more than a little alarmed at Sienna's forcefulness, I try to step around her so that I can grip the railing and pull myself up and away from her, but her grip intensifies.

'Get out of my way,' I say, through gritted teeth, my heart racing.

Is this what happened to Angelica?

I use both hands to grip the railing, but in doing so, Jake's phone begins to slip free from my sweaty grasp and I almost lose my footing trying to save it. It's only then that Sienna finally releases me.

It feels like slow motion as Jake's phone slips completely from my fingers and my hands claw the air for the railing.

'Sienna,' I cry, as I fall back.

But it's not Sienna who comes to my aid.

It's Jake who lunges down the steps and clamps his hands around my wrists. It's Jake who drags me up the steps to the safety of solid ground, where we both collapse onto the wet dirt beside the hatch, to catch our breaths in the howling wind.

'Your phone,' is the first thing I say, through a mouthful of my own hair.

Jake pats my shoulder and gives it a light squeeze. 'Don't worry. It's just a phone. I'm glad you're okay.'

Sienna emerges from the basement and stares down at me, her hands covering her mouth.

'What's your problem?' I ask, my heart still racing from the scare, my body shivering with shock.

'I'm so sorry, Maz. I didn't mean it. I was so worried about Lucas and... and I just don't know who to trust out here... I really don't. I wanted a better look around the basement because... I just know that something bad has happened to Lucas, I just know it.'

'If it wasn't for Jake...' I say, the words dying in my throat.

'I'm so sorry, Maz.'

Sienna bends down and wraps her arms around me, resting her head on my shoulder and that's when I realise where I've smelt her perfume before.

In Lance's car and on his shirt collar.

29

I run straight back to the house, despite Sienna calling my name. Although she sounds terrified and there's a pleading note to her voice, she can't be trusted anymore. I'm not sure that anybody here can.

Sienna and Lance? I can't imagine it.

There's a slim chance that this could be a coincidence. The same perfume can be worn by millions of women. But the odds that Sienna is the one who is wearing the exact scent… that and the fact that she is the one who took the photo that was printed and planted in my room… this is more than just a coincidence. For all I know Lucas going missing could be a carefully crafted move in Sienna's grand scheme for revenge.

But why? She was never particularly close to Angelica. There must be more to it, something behind all of this. Maybe she too had a secret crush on Samuel, but that's a stretch, because then that would have made the three of us, and she never showed any signs of stronger than normal feelings for Sam. If anything she hardly spoke to him much, only if I was around.

Unless Lizzie put her up to it. Tamara and Sienna have both mentioned that they kept in touch with Lizzie. Could this entire weekend be a set-up? Is Lizzie using Tamara and Sienna to get back at me for Angelica's death? That would explain why Sienna's perfume was all over Lance. Lizzie knew I was working as a waitress, who knows what else she knows about me? She probably found out about Lance and sent Sienna to do her dirty work. And now here I am, stuck in a remote location with them all.

I *need* to get out of here.

And as much as I'm annoyed with him and therefore don't want to rely on his help, I need Lance. He's the only one I can trust, maybe not to keep his pants on, but to keep me safe at least. We need to get our things, hop in the car and drive as far away from this house as possible. If we can't do that then I'm happy to trek through the bush just to get away from everyone.

The thought of getting out of here and leaving this place and my past behind me gives me an extra burst of energy. I quicken my pace and burst through the front door. When the wind slams it shut behind me I wince, but the house is still and quiet as I tiptoe through it. I keep expecting Sienna to show up, but nobody follows me through the front door. She's probably gone to search for Lizzie's dad's workshop herself, that's if it still exists. I'm not sure who to believe anymore. Because Sienna could have said that she saw it as a ruse to get me alone out there.

I head straight upstairs and open the bedroom door to hear the comforting sound of Lance's soft snoring. Outside the window, the night sky is growing lighter, the midnight blue fading to a purplish grey over the now calm and silvery ocean. At least the storm is well and truly over and it looks like tomorrow will bring much better weather, which means the track will likely dry up.

I don't bother to get changed into my pyjamas because I want to be ready to leave this place the second Lance pops his eyes open. But I decide it won't hurt to lie down for half an hour or so, just so that I can collect my thoughts.

As I slip into bed, Lance murmurs something in his sleep, something unintelligible. His forehead creases with dreamed-up worries so I slip my arm around his warm body to soothe him. Even though Lance is a lying cheat, I still care about him. I can't help it. I loved him once. Not as much as I loved Samuel – I don't think anyone can ever replace him – but I did love Lance in my own way.

My fingers brush something, a piece of paper, tucked near Lance's stomach. Lance makes a snuffling sound when I grab it but continues to breathe deeply and evenly. I sit up and reach for my phone and shine the torch light over the crumpled piece of paper in my hand.

You're going to lose him too

I gasp and Lance stirs. He blinks several times then looks up at me.

'Maz. Are you okay?' Lance sits up and rubs his face, then realisation dawns in his hazel eyes and he groans and drops his shoulders. 'Shit, I'm such an idiot. I'm sorry about before.' He shakes his head. 'I really am.'

'It's okay,' I say, not even caring about the Lizzie thing anymore. 'Don't worry about that. Let's just work out how we're going to get out of here.'

Lance looks at me, his mouth opening slightly, as though he's hesitant to speak his mind.

'If it's about that photo... I honestly don't think it's malicious.' He raises his brows. 'To tell you the truth I just think there may be a bit of... jealously... or at least rivalry between you girls.'

'Can I ask you something?'

The bed squeaks as Lance shifts around on the mattress. He sighs and half-smiles, but I can tell that he's bothered by the idea of being questioned because of the rigidness of his body and the way that he keeps avoiding my gaze.

'Sure. Go ahead.'

'Have you ever met Sienna before?'

Lance meets my eyes. 'Sienna? Not before today.'

'Are you absolutely sure?'

Lance takes my hand and looks me straight in the eye.

'I've never met her outside this place. I swear on my life.'

I nod, unsure if Lance is telling the truth or if he's gotten especially good at lying. But it doesn't really matter. What matters is getting out of here as quickly as possible.

'Okay. One more question.'

He swallows thickly but nods.

I shine my torchlight at his bedside table.

'Is that your notebook and pen?'

Lance glances at it and hangs his head. 'Yeah.'

My heart pounds as I slide off the mattress and get to my feet.

'Did you write this?'

I hold up the note I found.

Lance drops his face into his hands and groans. 'Yes. I wrote the note. I tried to disguise my writing so that you wouldn't know that it was me.'

The skin at the back of my neck prickles.

'Why would you do that?' I take a step back so that I'm closer to the door. 'Are you responsible for the photo too?'

Lance gets to his feet and raises his palms in the air, his eyes wide in alarm.

'No. Of course not. I've never seen that photo in my life.' He rubs his face again. 'Don't you get it, Maz? I wrote that note because... because I thought if I could get you worried about me, then your old feelings might creep back and we might stand a chance in... in getting back together.' He scratches the back of his head and meets my gaze. 'It's stupid, okay, I get it. I'm pathetic.'

I stare at Lance long and hard, studying the stoop in his shoulders, and the way he hangs his head. My stupid heart can't help but soften with sympathy. The fact that he went to the trouble to make it look as though his life was being threatened, just so that I could care more about him, is oddly touching in a mildly disturbing way.

'It's okay,' I say, palms up. 'I get it. But you scared the hell out of me and I'm already freaked out about the photo, so can we not pull these kinds of pranks anymore? We need to be a team.'

Lance closes the distance between us and nods rapidly. 'Yes. A team. You and me.'

'Good. Now we need to focus on getting out of here. Because I'm running out of people I can trust.'

Lance sighs. 'You mean people like me, don't you?'

I sigh. My ex-boyfriend can be completely draining when he's in victim mode. 'We're a team, remember? So let's act like one. Come on. Let's come up with a plan.' I sit down and pat the edge of the mattress so that Lance can join me.

We talk quietly, making plans to walk and leave Lance's car behind until it's safe to come back and get it. Lance isn't exactly joyful about the idea but he shares my fears about staying so he doesn't exactly complain too much either.

Dawn arrives, bringing with it a soft lilac sky and the sound of birds singing, heralding a brand new, brighter day ahead.

Lance falls back against the soft mattress and closes his eyes. I'm tempted to do the same. Just for a few minutes. After setting an alarm on my phone, I curl up beside him. My lids flutter closed at the sound of a particularly uplifting birdsong and to Lance's soft snores.

But before I manage to fall into a deep sleep, my eyes snap open to the sound of shouting coming from downstairs.

I sit up and strain my ears.

'What's going on?' Lance asks, groggy with sleep.

'It sounds like Lizzie and Tamara.' I spring out of bed, adrenaline whooshing through my veins. 'We have to go check it out.'

Lance sighs dramatically then reluctantly drags himself out of bed.

30

Lance grips my hand tightly and breathes against my neck as we take the stairs as quietly as possible. I do my best to listen in, ears strained, breath held, but when a step creaks beneath us, the intense conversation comes to an abrupt halt.

'Who's there?' Lizzie calls out.

Lance shakes his head at me but I give his hand a sharp tug.

'It's me, Maz, and Lance.'

As we enter the kitchen, the conflict between Tamara and Lizzie simmers somewhat but the air still crackles with tension.

'Is everything okay?' I ask, my throat raw and my voice raspy from being awake for most of the night.

Tamara stands at the sink, a glass of water in hand, her head down. Has she been crying?

Lizzie pours boiling water from the kettle into a mug with a picture of an orange cat on it. 'Sienna, Jake and Lucas are all missing. I was grilling Tamara about it. Something is up,' says Lizzie, setting the kettle down. She throws me a pointed glance, while she vigorously dunks her teabag in and out of the steaming mug.

'Yeah, something *is* up.' Tamara sets down her water and turns to face us, her arms folded across her ample chest. 'And we should be asking Lizzie about it. She's the one who organised this trip.'

Lizzie squeezes the steaming teabag between her fingers and leaves it on the sink. 'I was hoping we'd get closure… and know the truth about what happened. Isn't that what everyone wants?' She cradles the mug between her skeletal fingers and takes a sip of tea.

'Jake wouldn't have left me.' Tamara's eyes fill with tears. 'We're engaged. He would have taken me with him. Something's wrong.'

'Yes, something is very wrong. Sienna and Lucas both went missing while Jake was around. Seems a little coincidental doesn't it?' Lizzie narrows her lavender eyes at Tamara and blows the curls of steam from the surface of her tea then takes another sip.

'What the hell is that supposed to mean? Why would Jake have anything to do with those two going missing?' Tamara puts her hands on her hips. 'What have you got against my boyfriend?'

'I'm just pointing out the coincidence of him being nearby when they both disappeared.' Lizzie clears her throat. 'Will also pointed out something interesting to me. My pain medication has gone missing, but I didn't know this because somebody went into my bathroom and replaced my pills with something else. The replacement pills look almost identical to what I take, but mine are pale blue in colour whereas the others are white. I didn't notice – probably because of all the candlelight, until Will pointed it out.'

'Are you serious?' I ask. I'm horrified. Who would do something so terrible?

'Will noticed I was acting strangely so he checked my meds. Turns out I've been taking something that's making me act out of character. Maybe you'd be able to enlighten me, Tams?'

'Enlighten you about what? I didn't even know you were taking pills until now.' Tamara shivers. 'But that's horrible though. Who would do something like that?' She looks at me and Lance.

'Hey, don't look at us.' Lance shuffles closer to my side.

Lizzie takes another sip of tea before setting it down and addressing us all. The morning light has cast a halo around her head, giving her buzz cut an ethereal glow. The visible scar gives her both an air of vulnerability as well as an underlying aura of strength.

'I don't know who to trust anymore, so I say we stick together from now on,' Lizzie says. 'If one of us wants to leave the house, we all leave together.'

'Good idea,' Lance says.

'Yeah. That's a great idea,' Tamara says. She comes to stand by my side. 'I say we go out and search for the others right now. Together.'

Lizzie nods. 'Wait. First I need to have a word with Maz. Alone.'

Tamara and Lance close in around me, as though I need protection from Lizzie.

'Anything you say to Maz, you can say in front of us,' says Tamara.

Lizzie's cheeks tint pink. 'Okay then. Well, Maz, I just want to apologise for the way I've been behaving this weekend. I haven't been myself. But I can't blame my behaviour entirely on the mixed medication. There are other things you need to know.'

'What things?'

Tamara stiffens beside me. 'Don't trust her, Maz. She's got some vendetta against you. She told me. When we first made contact a few years ago she told me how much she's hated you since that day.'

'I told you that in confidence,' Lizzie says, then she puts a hand to her mouth and looks at me. 'I'm sorry, Maz. I know it looks bad...' She shakes her head. 'And yeah, I may have said that I hated you. But that was when I was looking for someone to blame for what happened to Angelica.'

I shrug. 'Don't feel too bad. I've always blamed myself for what happened anyway.'

Lizzie takes a step closer to me. 'Wait, so it's true then?'

'What's true?' Lance asks.

'That Maz tried to steal Samuel away from Angelica,' says Lizzie, her voice soft and her eyes staring into nothingness. 'That she told him she loved him and when he didn't return her feelings she got angry and pushed Angelica down the basement stairs.' Lizzie's gaze hardens as her focus returns and she turns her attention back to me. 'So Tamara was right all along.'

Lance takes a step back and eyes me warily. Surely he doesn't think I'm capable of hurting another human being.

'What?' I turn to look at Tamara whose cheeks have flushed pink. 'Why do you keep pointing the finger at me?'

Tamara opens her mouth to speak but then closes it.

I turn back to Lizzie. 'None of what she is saying is true. Did Tamara tell you that she came running out onto the beach the night they died? Crying?'

'Wait, you didn't tell me that,' says Lizzie, staring at Tamara. 'Why were you crying?'

Tamara's face turns bright red, but she says nothing.

'And anyway,' I say, looking at Lizzie, 'you were the one who wanted to meet me in the basement, that's the only reason I found them, and you weren't even there. Where were you? Why did you want me to come to the basement?'

Lizzie stares at me, stunned. 'What are you talking about?' she whispers.

'When I saw Tamara on the beach that night, she told me that you asked me to meet you there. So, I went and... and I found them like that.' Tears burn the backs of my eyes but I force them to retreat. This is not the time to collapse into a heap, not when I'm finally getting to say my piece.

'Wait, you didn't tell me that,' says Lizzie, staring at Tamara. 'Why were you crying? And why did you tell Maz to go to the basement? I didn't ask you to say that. Why would you make something like that up?'

I back away from everyone and Tamara looks at me.

'Maz, wait. I'm sorry for accusing you. This place, and everything that's been happening has freaked me out.' She nods towards Lizzie. 'She's not right in the head. She's lying. She did ask me to tell you to meet her in the basement. I swear to you. She's lying. Maybe she's lying about where Sienna is too. Maybe the two of them are in on this.'

The perfume comes to mind. But I just can't seem to find a connection between Sienna and Lance and what happened that night.

Lance looks at us all, his face pale, and makes a T-shape with his hands. 'Okay, this is getting way too intense. Time out. We can stand here all morning throwing accusations around, but the fact is, we have three missing people who disappeared during one hell of a storm last night. There could be a reasonable explanation for all this.'

When none of us respond, he shakes his head and marches over to the front door. 'Well, I'm not going to waste any more time. I'm heading out to search.'

'Lance is right,' says Tamara. 'Let's put our differences aside for now. Once we've found everyone, maybe we can sit down and have an adult conversation about this.'

'So you're saying I should simply forget that you've been going around accusing me of murder?' Lizzie says, glaring at Tamara.

'I could say the same,' I add.

'I never said that. You have to believe me, Maz.' Tamara shakes her head and looks at Lizzie, who seems to have turned extra pale.

'Are you okay, Lizzie?' I ask, taking a cautious step towards her.

Lizzie flutters her lashes and grips the kitchen counter.

'Yeah, just a dizzy spell.' She looks me in the eye and shuffles back a step, as though she's frightened of me. 'I'm good. But I'm going to walk behind everyone. Because I'm not sure who to trust right now.'

'But how can we be sure to trust you?' Tamara asks, narrowing her gaze.

Lance swings the front door open and we all cringe from the bright sunshine like vampires after so long in the darkness.

'The track will dry up today,' Lance says.

The possibility of getting home by the end of today fills me with a renewed sense of hope. Maybe everything will turn out okay. This afternoon could very well be the start of a new life for me.

Tamara looks at Lance as she follows him outside. 'We're running out of time.'

'What do you mean? Running out of time for what?' I ask, feeling a prickle of unease creep up the back of my neck.

'Meaning we need to find them so we can all go home by the time the track dries up. I don't want to spend another second here,' she says with a shudder, her voice hysterical.

Lizzie grabs my hand after we walk through the door and tugs me away from the others so that I walk beside her. I'm not sure that I'm comfortable being so close to her, but with Lance only a few meters away, I guess I'm fairly safe.

'I never asked Tamara to tell you to meet me in the basement. That's a lie. Don't trust her, Maz. Something isn't right with Tamara. Just look at her hair – she used to be blonde like me, but now she's brunette – and her *boobs*. She's trying to be *you*... I think she's obsessed with you.'

I keep my voice low so that Tamara and Lance don't overhear us. 'She was actually obsessed with Samuel back in the day.'

'Sam?' Lizzie blinks rapidly. 'She never told me. But then again, neither did you.'

'She was madly in love with him.'

'Tamara in love with Samuel?' Lizzie grows quiet and her lavender eyes darken. 'That explains why Angelica said she'd been catching Tamara staring at her a lot around the time. It was starting to make her feel uncomfortable.' Lizzie puts a hand to her mouth. 'Oh God, and I brushed it off and told her not to worry. Oh no, what if...' Lizzie's voice trails off and she shakes her head, unwilling to believe what she's thinking.

My eyes are drawn to the tiny, pale, hairlike scars across Lizzie's thin wrists and I think about what Tamara said, about Lizzie spending time in a mental institution. Poor Lizzie. She's gone through a lot. Maybe reconnecting with Tamara and Sienna only made her mental condition worse. Maybe that's why she called us here on this holiday, because she's unable to put it behind her and let what happened rest.

'Let's search that old workshop,' Lance calls over his shoulder. 'Maybe they're in there.'

Tamara quickens her steps behind him, struggling over the sand dunes to keep up.

'I thought your dad's workshop had been torn down?' I ask Lizzie as we quicken our pace, the sand punishing my ankles. I've never been one for exercise but now I wish I was. I could do with some extra fitness right now.

'Why would it be torn down? It's got a bit of white-ant damage but it was my dad's favourite place. I go there to write poetry when I'm feeling down and to feel close to him. I would never tear it down. Dad was the last one to touch it so I want to keep it as he left it.' She frowns as she catches her breath. 'Who told you it had been torn down?'

I look up at Tamara who is already entering the bushes up ahead while Lance hangs back waiting for us.

'Tamara. Why would she say that when it's not true?'

'Let me go ahead first, to make sure that it's safe,' says Lance. 'I'll call out to you.' He leaves the beach and disappears into the bush.

We slow down a little, my entire body prickling with apprehension. What if Tamara has Jake waiting in the bushes, ready to pounce on Lance?

Or what if this is Lizzie's plan all along? Maybe she has Will waiting in the shed for us all. To do what, I'm not sure.

'Where's Will?' I ask.

Lizzie's face pales and she looks at the damp sand beneath our feet. 'He left this morning.'

'By car? Is the track dry already?'

'No. On foot.'

'Why would he do that? Did you two fight?'

'That's another thing we need to talk about.' She gnaws on her bottom lip, then shakes her head and nods at the bushes. 'I'll tell you later, when we're alone. Come on, let's go. Nobody had better touch any of my dad's stuff or I'll be pissed.'

'Lance told us to wait,' I say, touching her arm. 'Tell me what happened with Will?'

'Okay. Well. He's not really my boyfriend.'

I nod. 'I didn't really feel a couple vibe between you two.'

'Yeah, well. I'm a bit embarrassed to say it, but I hired him to pretend to be my boyfriend for the weekend. He's an escort and needs the money to help care for his sick father. I met him through a friend of a friend and when I told Tamara about him she convinced me to hire him for the weekend.'

'Why?'

'Because although Tamara kept saying all this horrible stuff about you, I wasn't ready to believe it. She convinced me that if I hired Will and set him up to seduce you, then it would prove that you were someone of ill morals, a boyfriend stealer.' Lizzie shakes her head. 'It all sounds so ridiculous now. Maybe Tamara is the one who's been switching my meds. I can't be sure though. My brain feels super foggy still.'

A shriek pierces the air, cutting through the quiet of the morning. A flock of gulls rise from the shore in the distance and circle the sky to land a little further away from us.

'That was Tamara!'

Lizzie grips my arm. 'Let's stay together. Don't leave me, Maz.' She points to the strip of tin roof visible through the trees and puts a finger to her lips and whispers, 'Follow me.'

Lizzie bends branches aside to allow me safe passage, but scratchy leaves still find their way, scraping against my arms and face. We come to a halt as we reach a clearing and find ourselves standing in front of Lizzie's dad's workshop, which is built out of sheet metal and wood and is the size of a double garage.

'Lance? Tamara?' says Lizzie.

Silence greets us, followed by the sound of the morning breeze gently rustling the leaves on the trees and shrubs that surround us.

'Tamara,' Lizzie whispers. 'Where are you?'

'Maybe they're inside,' I say, my heart hammering against my chest, my pulse deafening in my ears. There must be some explanation behind the fact that everyone keeps vanishing into thin air.

Lizzie approaches the door, her thin, elegant hand on the handle. We don't say a word to each other, we don't need to communicate the terror we're both feeling right now. I put a hand on her bony shoulder and give it a gentle squeeze and she nods before twisting the knob and opening the door.

Lizzie takes one step forward, freezes and makes a strange sound in her throat, halfway between a groan and a gasp.

I step around her so that I can see whatever it is with my own eyes and gasp with horror when I see Sienna and Lucas, so pale they appear blue, their eyes open and staring vacantly ahead, their lifeless bodies in macabre positions.

31

Jake steps out from the shadowy corner of the workshop, palms up, his face a mask of concern and his black eyepatch fixed firmly in place. What's the deal with the eyepatch if he doesn't need it?

Lizzie screams as he shuffles closer.

'Calm down. Just calm down, please,' Jake says.

I force my gaze to sweep over Sienna and Lucas once more, to be sure that they're dead, and all the blood drains from my head to my feet.

'What did you do to them?' I ask.

'It wasn't me. I found them like this.' Jake's single eye flickers down to the bodies briefly before he coughs and then gags and has to turn his head. 'I brought them here. Alive. Lucas was passed out when Sienna came… but she just kept screaming so I left her here and locked the door.' He swallows down what appears to be a sob. 'I planned to find Lance, ask him what to do, but I couldn't find him and by the time I came back she was dead.'

Lizzie sways on her feet so I slip my arm around her waist to steady her.

'Are you going to kill us?' she asks, her voice whisper-quiet.

Jake shakes his head. 'No. No of course not. I'm not a killer.' He paces the floor and puts both hands to his head. 'I'm not a killer. I didn't do it. I swear.'

Lizzie backs away from him, dragging me with her, and once we're outside of the shed I gulp down a lungful of fresh air, grateful that I don't have to look at the dead bodies anymore.

Bile rises up my throat as I think about their vacant eyes, all the life inside of them gone, the disturbing angle of their necks. No longer Sienna and Lucas. Bodies. That's all they are now. Dead things.

'Where's Tamara?' Lizzie asks, when Jake follows us outside.

'With Lance.'

'Where'd they go?' I ask. 'What did you do to them? We heard her scream.'

Jake glances at me and as I back away from him, I realise that Lizzie is no longer standing behind me. Did she manage to slip away? If she did then hopefully she'll manage to get help. I try my best not to think about how long it will take for her to reach the main road.

'You need to stay calm,' says Jake, his palms out again. 'I'm not going to hurt you.'

I cry out for Lance.

'He's not going to help you,' Jake says, shaking his head.

I take several steps back before I turn to run, but immediately freeze when I almost bump into Lance, who's holding Lizzie. He has one arm around her waist and a hand clamped over her mouth.

Tamara comes to stand beside them, hands on her hips. She looks fine. Unhurt. Then why did she scream?

'You nearly let her get away,' Tamara says to Jake.

Lizzie's eyes bulge at me and she makes a sound behind Lance's hand.

'Let her go, Lance,' I say, my heart drumming against my chest. 'Why are you doing this?'

Lance doesn't respond. Instead he glares at me. There's a hard glint in his eyes that I don't recognise.

'Tams, this needs to end now.' The gruff threat in Lance's voice chills my blood. 'Get your phone out and get the confession.'

'Wait. You two know each other?'

Lance sighs, clearly frustrated. 'If you want to spare Lizzie's life, I need you to confess.'

'To what?' I stare at the both of them, completely confused.

Lance throws a death stare Tamara's way. 'You'd better not have been shitting me this whole time.'

'I haven't.' Tamara licks her lips and tucks her trembling hands behind her back. 'Maz did it. She's the one.'

'She's the one what? What did I do?'

The veins on the back of Lance's hand bulge as he tightens his grip on Lizzie who screams against his fingers.

'Who killed my sister,' he says.

'What? What do you mean? You told me that you're an only child and that your parents died in a car accident.'

'Only child, hey?' says Jake, looking offended.

'It was part of the act, okay.' Lance rolls his eyes at Jake.

Lizzie groans and her knees buckle so that Lance has to hold her up.

'She can't breathe,' I say. 'Let her go, Lance. Please. We can talk this out, whatever it is.'

'Talk it out?' Lance makes a face. 'What is wrong with you? You think you can just kill an innocent girl and just go on with your life as though nothing happened?'

My mind goes straight to Angelica. But Angelica was an only child too. She didn't have any siblings.

'I didn't kill anyone.'

Tamara's eyes flicker nervously from me to Lizzie.

'She's lying,' she says to Lance.

'Someone's lying,' says Jake, who glares pointedly at Tamara.

'Tamara, you need to do something, help us. You can't let Lizzie get hurt,' I plead.

'It's her own fault.' Tamara shakes her head, her green eyes widening in a way that makes her look unhinged. 'She's been an absolute pain in the arse. She had one job, but she messed it all up for us.'

'*Us?* How do you all know each other? How do you know Lance?'

Tamara's gaze shoots to Jake first, then rests on Lance, but she remains silent.

I turn to Jake. 'Can you please explain to me what's going on here?'

'Jake is my brother,' says Lance, before Jake gets to speak. 'I had a sister too, but she died. She was murdered.' He tightens his grip on Lizzie who looks ready to faint again.

My scalp prickles as I meet Lance's gaze. 'How did she die?'

'You know how she died because you're the one who did it.'

I take a step back as he drags Lizzie along with him towards me.

'Stop lying and admit the truth,' he growls, baring his teeth. 'Tams! Get your phone out and press record. Maz is about to confess to the murder of my sister and the police will finally be able to solve this case.'

'What… what do you mean?'

'The case. It's unsolved.' Lance shakes his head at me like I'm some kind of dimwit. 'And because of that Angelica's assets have been frozen. Did you know that she had a fortune sitting in a bank account waiting for her on her eighteenth birthday? Which was, incidentally, only two weeks away from the day she died.'

I nod. We all knew about Angelica's inheritance from her insanely rich mother who had died of an overdose of painkillers when Angelica was only ten years old. Her stepfather was in charge of the funds until she came of age. But that didn't happen. And then her stepfather died of a heart attack not long after he learnt of Angelica's tragic death.

'So until they solve the case, everything that is rightly mine is frozen.'

'Wait, so you and Jake are brothers?' I shake my head. 'Angelica would have told us that she had two brothers.'

'Jake and I first met at an orphanage when we were little boys and were lucky enough to be adopted into the same family,' Lance says with a sneer. 'But Angelica and I, we share the same mother, the same blood. I was given up at birth. Too much for a spoilt sixteen-year-old to bear. Even though two years later she was more than happy to keep my sister and raise her as a bratty princess.'

My throat tightens. 'Angelica was never bratty. She was the most beautiful and kind person.'

'Then why did you kill her?'

'I didn't. She must have fallen.'

Lance shakes his head and looks at Tamara. 'Go on, tell her we know the truth, that you told us what she confessed.'

'I didn't tell you anything,' I say, spitting my words out at Tamara, a fire growing in my belly. 'Why are you lying?'

'Make her tell us.' Lance glares at Tamara. 'Shove that phone in her face. Now.'

Tamara swipes and taps at her phone, then holds it towards me with trembling fingers.

'Tell them, Maz,' she says, unable to meet my gaze. 'About... about how you pushed Angelica and how you also put something in Samuel's drink. That you did it all because you were mad... mad because after you confessed to Samuel that you loved him, he didn't love you back.'

'What?' I'd laugh out loud at the absurdity of it all if it weren't for the fact that Sienna and Lucas's dead bodies are lying only metres away from us.

'It's true,' says Tamara, her voice coming out choked. 'Maz ruined everything. We were going to start a life together. He loved me. I was waiting on the beach for him... and he never came because she killed him.'

'*I* was waiting for Sam on the beach. You're crazy, Tamara, and you're a liar.'

Lizzie starts to struggle in Lance's grip. She mumbles something behind his hand and he surprises us all by removing it and allowing her to speak.

'Make it quick,' he says, 'because I'm sick of this timewasting.'

Lizzie catches her breath and then lunges for Tamara. Despite Lizzie's weakness, Lance has to drag her back and keep her at bay.

'You told me that Samuel killed himself after he found Angelica dead,' Lizzie says. 'You didn't say that Maz put something in his drink. You've changed your story.'

Tamara glances at Jake and then Lance and takes a step back. 'She's making this up.'

'No. No I'm not,' says Lizzie, and I see a spark in her eyes that's been missing this entire trip. The same spark that used to fire up her eyes ten years ago. 'She's been lying to you this whole time. I bet she's lying about who killed Angelica too. I bet she did it herself.'

32

'Speaking of lying.' Tamara gnaws on her bottom lip and meets my gaze. 'You want to meet Cameron? The guy Angelica was supposedly writing to and cheating on Samuel with?'

My blood runs cold as Tamara nods in the direction of Lance.

'That's Cameron. Lance Cameron. Turns out he wasn't her lover. He's her brother.' She sneers at me. 'Lance has been lying to you this whole time. He's never loved you, he's only been dating you because he thinks you murdered his sister.'

Lance glares at Tamara, then angrily clamps his hand back over Lizzie's mouth and holds her tighter. 'Okay, enough. Start confessing, Maz, or Lizzie will join your friends in the shed.'

'But I didn't kill her. I didn't kill Samuel either,' I say. 'I loved him. That part is true. We loved *each other.* That photo you saw last night, that was the moment we declared our love to each other. Why would I murder the guy I was in love with? Tamara is lying to you.'

Lance growls with frustration. He regards Tamara, who stands there clutching the phone, her eyes to the ground.

'We should never have trusted the word of a girl from a mental institution,' he spits.

'Shut up,' says Jake, his face red with rage. 'If you call Tamara mental, you're calling me mental.'

'You spent half a year in the nuthouse, of course you're mental,' says Lance, with a laugh and a shake of his head.

Jake rushes forward, his fists raised. 'So help me I'll smash your face in if you don't shut up.'

Lance drags Lizzie back along with him. 'Woah, settle down, bro. You don't want to accidentally hit Lizzie here.'

'I will not settle down. We've got two dead bodies in that shed and no confession. We're going to end up in jail because of your screw-up.'

Lance glares at Jake. 'I only tried to shut them up a little. It's not my fault I don't know my own strength and they fucking died.'

'Wait.' I look at Tamara. 'I thought you said that it was Lizzie who spent time in a mental institution and that you visited her there.'

Lizzie reacts by flailing in Lance's arms and screaming against his hand.

Lance shakes his head, a huge grin on his lips. 'My brother met your friend Tams while he was in the mental home. She lived there, as a resident. My adoptive parents had Jake locked up because of that stupid patch he started wearing as a teen. They thought he was going nuts. Mum thought he wanted to become a pirate.'

'You know that's not why I wear it.' Jake's face is red and his lone eye murderously fixed on Lance.

'But you said that Lizzie spent time in a mental institution,' I say, looking at Tamara. 'You said that she lost weight and started cutting herself and tried to commit suicide after her dad died.'

Lizzie thrashes against Lance's tight hold and glares at Tamara.

Lance raises his brows at Lizzie, appearing amused, and removes his hand from her mouth again.

'I'm vegan now, that's why I'm a lot skinnier, plus I own and run a flower farm. These cuts are from the sharp thorns when I harvest roses.'

Lance covers her mouth before she can say any more. But I don't need to hear another word because I believe Lizzie.

'This is getting nowhere,' Lance says growling with impatience. 'I need a confession if I want to ride off into the sunset a rich and happy man.'

'With me by your side,' Tamara says, coming to plant a kiss on Lance's cheek.

Lance looks at Jake, who's taking this all in, and grins at the surprise and hurt in his brother's single blue eye.

'So now *you* have a problem, Jake,' says Lance. 'You need to get a confession out of Maz before we kill her... or else you'll be going to jail for the whole lot.' He grins wickedly. 'It's up to you how you squeeze a confession out of her, bro. Remove her fingernails or something.' Lance winks at Jake. 'Think of the bullies who used to bash you in high school if you have to, because if you don't force a confession out of her, I'm going to have to kill you both and write a confessional suicide note on your behalf, little bro.'

'You fucking bastard,' says Jake, his face red and coated with sweat. 'I bet Tams was the one who killed your sister.'

I look at Lance and realise that Tamara isn't standing by his side anymore. Lizzie's eyes bulge as she stares in horror at something just over my shoulder.

My scalp prickles and my blood runs cold as I turn to see Tamara standing behind me, carrying a shovel in her hand.

'You killed them. It was all you. The moment you interfered with my plans you handed them their death sentence.'

Tamara's eyes are crazed as she raises the shovel over her head.

I cringe, cross my arms over my face and shuffle back, but I'm not quick enough.

'It's all your fault,' she shrieks as she swings the shovel at my head.

Before I can scream, everything turns black.

33

Then

Tamara

'Meet me in the basement in ten minutes. There's something I need to tell you. It's important,' I add, which changes the disinterested, distracted look on Samuel's face to interested.

'Is it about Maz?' he asks, his blue eyes flickering to life.

'Umm… yeah,' I lie. Anything to get him alone. But once we are together, and he sees all the effort I've gone to in getting ready for him, then he'll forget all about Maz and her whiney, needy ways. I mean, can she not leave him alone for a second? It's Samuel this and Samuel that. I know they're best friends, but how's the guy supposed to get a life with her constantly hovering over him.

'Is she okay?' Sam blinks at me and sways on his feet. I think he might be drunk. Oh well, all the better.

'She's fine,' I say, not even bothering to hide my irritation at all the Maz talk. Sam's too drunk to notice anyway.

'Did she…' Sam pauses and glances over his shoulder towards the living room where everyone is sitting in a circle taking shots and engaging in the world's most disgusting game of strip poker. Gross. Who on earth wants to see Brayden naked? If Sam were playing, then that would be a totally different story. I'd be the first to put my hand up if that were the case. 'Did she tell you... about what happened?'

My pulse drums loudly in my ears. 'Yeah... she told me.' I'm not sure if I'm supposed to appear happy or sad or mad about it so I keep my face neutral because I'm frickin clueless at this point. 'But anyway, basement in ten minutes. Just you.'

Samuel's face turns grim. 'It's not anything bad, is it?' he asks, tilting his head to the side.

I offer him a huge, reassuring smile, hoping that it's not making my big nose jut out. 'It's good. It's very good. You'll see.'

Samuel raises his brows at that and a small, feint smile rises and abolishes all that seriousness away. 'Okay. See you in ten.' He slaps my shoulder like I see the boys do after a game of footy and it irks me that he's treating me like one of the boys.

But once I'm alone in the bedroom, stuffing my empty bra with my new cup fillers and wearing the stunning new dress I spent three pay packets on – red because apparently guys find girls more sexually attractive when dressed in this particular colour – I'm feeling much more confident.

'Goodbye, Angelica and Maz; hello, Tamara,' I whisper to my reflection in the mirror. I dab on some lipstick in the shade of Amore – also red of course – and spritz my favourite perfume all over me; then before I leave the room, I remember the sachets I especially ordered from overseas for this very trip.

I carefully tear open the pink one and tip its contents into a cup of water on my bedside table, stir it and down the contents. Yuk. It tastes chalky. Then I take the blue one and pop it in my overstuffed bra for Samuel. I'm hoping all those rave reviews online about the powders are legitimate because I *need* this to work.

I take one last look in the mirror, to see if the stuff has magically transformed me already somehow. But I look exactly the same. Then again, I don't exactly need a love potion because I'm already madly in love with Sam. But still, the instructions were that we're both to take the powder. Maybe it'll take effect after we've both had our doses.

I hum a romantic song to myself as I breeze past the others who are too distracted watching Brayden gyrate around the living room wearing someone's red lacy G-string, which is probably Lizzie's.

Once outside, a cool breeze tickles my hair. I can't believe that it's finally happening. That I've mustered up the courage to do this. And the bonus is, it looks like I've gotten in before Maz. She hasn't got anyone fooled. Everyone knows she's madly and obsessively in love with Samuel.

I giggle to myself. Oh my God, the look on her face when Sam and I tell her that we're going to be together. Angelica's face too. But she probably won't care because she's too busy writing to her side piece, Cameron.

I go around the side of the house and a muffled cheer erupts from inside. Eww, that was probably Brayden taking off the G-string.

Focus, Tamara.

I shake my head free of any revolting visuals and bend down to open the hatch. I slowly raise it, but it still screeches and I wince, hoping that nobody from inside heard me. The last thing I need is nosy Maz to come down and interrupt Sam and me.

I'm extra careful in my three-inch heels as I take the stairs, noticing that the light in the basement is already on. Damn. I hope it's not Lizzie. That'll really screw things up. She'll make me a laughing stock and tell everyone back at the house before I even get the chance to speak to Samuel, and by then I'll probably just give up.

'Oh,' I say, surprised to find that Samuel is already here, early, sitting at a small table on a wooden chair with a glass of something – rum and cola by the looks of it – while he writes something in his journal.

It's something I'd kill to read, Sam's own inner thoughts. Gosh, I'd memorise every word. But, if we're going to work as a couple, then I need to allow him his privacy. A good girlfriend doesn't go snooping around in her boyfriend's things. I'm not going to be the kind of girl that demands to see his phone or anything like that. Of course, I'll make sure that I delete Maz's details first, because we won't need to keep in touch with her or with anyone from the group after leavers'. I mean, it's time to move on and live our lives. They're all getting annoying anyway.

Sam is enough. He's all I need.

'Hey, Tams. I came down right away. Thought I'd get some writing done.'

I nod, wondering if he's writing about me.

'About me, is it?' I put a hand to my Amore-coated lips, unable to believe that I just uttered those words. Oh well. I add what I hope is a sexy, flirtatious smile. I may as well go the whole hog and throw myself into this.

Samuel's smile drops and his face grows serious, a furrow etched deep in his brow. Sam is just about perfect, the perfect guy for me anyway, but being gloomy and depressed all the time is his one failing. Hopefully once we're a couple I can snap him out of it.

'You're all dressed up,' he says. 'Is everyone going into town?'

My cheeks heat up as I glance down at the hem of my dress, which I don't have to look too far down for because it's practically at the very top of my thighs.

Don't falter, Tams, keep going. You can do this.

'Can't a girl get spruced up for a boy?' I say, lowering my voice, trying to sound flirtatious again, but I know it's not working because Sam is looking increasingly worried. My entire face and neck burns with embarrassment. I probably look like a tomato, which is what Maz looked like after being out in the sun earlier today.

Sam thinks for a minute, frowning, then his entire face relaxes. 'Oh wow. I didn't know you and Brayden were a thing.' He gives me a warm smile and shakes his head. 'Good for you, Tamara.'

I don't like the way he says it, like I'm slow or something and he's really happy that someone like me has managed to do the unachievable and find myself a boyfriend.

Why does nothing ever go to plan for me? Those stupid law of attraction books tell me to visualise and all I do is visualise Samuel and I together. Sam and I holding hands. Sam and I laughing together. Sam and I kissing. Sam and I having sex. So why isn't he rushing to help me down the stairs and throwing his arms around me in a loving embrace?

'Umm, I'd never go for a guy like Brayden. He's disgusting. No way,' I say, putting a little flirt back into my voice as I finally take the last step. I move as sexily as I can in these ridiculous, toothpick heels towards Samuel, swaying my non-existent hips, the chicken fillets jiggling around in my bra cups, hopefully in a realistic way.

'Oh. But you said…' Samuel's voice trails off and I can see the moment when it finally hits home, because his entire body stiffens and he shifts his gaze to the table. His shyness and vulnerability makes him even more attractive.

'My kind of guy is the kind that is thoughtful, kind, he's a thinker, he…' I stare down at Sam's journal when I reach the table. 'He writes.'

Samuel's cheeks flush pink. He brings the drink to his lips and takes a sip, his hands trembling. I wonder if he'd notice if I poured the contents of the blue sachet into his drink right now.

He clears his throat. 'You don't mean... you don't mean me, do you?'

My skin prickles at the way he's speaking, as though he's mildly horrified at the thought of being the object of my affections.

'Yes. Of course I mean you.' I'm not sure what to do right now, my heart is practically clawing its way out of my chest and up my neck, and I feel the urge to slap some sense into Samuel. But of course I can't do that.

Act, Tamara. Think. What would Angelica or Maz do? Or Lizzie? They'd play it cool, that's what.

So I giggle, even though I feel like a complete idiot doing it, then lean forward to rest my hands against the desk, hoping that the bra stuffers are giving me a nice cleavage even if it's fake. But Sam isn't even looking at me, he's staring at the open pages of his journal.

I glance down and spy Maz's name scribbled about twenty times across the pages, beside lots of little squiggly love hearts, and a swell of anger rises in my chest, making me feel hot – not sexy-hot, but angry-hot.

'Oh.' Samuel closes his journal and rises from his seat. 'I'm sorry, Tams... you're... you're a great girl, you really are, but... I'm in love with someone else.'

Everything stops, even my heart, because it's got to be broken after that. Shattered.

Suddenly the cup fillers and the makeup and the dress feel utterly ridiculous, like I'm a little girl dressing up in her mum's clothes trying to impress the adults. But the difference is that I'm not a cute kid – I've never been the cute one, and no one is smiling at me. In fact, Sam looks terrified of me, and that's not how you want the person you love looking at you.

'If I'm so great, then why aren't I good enough for you?'

Sam frowns and clutches the journal to his chest, then blinks and sways on his feet.

'It's not about being good enough. Of course you are. But my heart is taken… that's all. It's nothing personal.' His eyes light up. 'I'm in love, Tamara. Really in love. I have been all along. Maz is… she's my soulmate.'

I see red. How dare Maz, who is supposed to be my friend, come and steal my guy behind my back?

'Sam? What are you guys doing down here?'

I jump at the voice coming from the open hatch. Bloody Angelica. She's going to ruin everything. I still have the little sachet of love potion… I just need to slip it in his drink and then everything will turn out fine.

'Angelica,' Sam calls. 'I'm just coming up.' He reaches for his drink.

'Wait. Don't touch it,' I say. 'Don't finish your drink. There's more I need to tell you… about Maz. She asked me to… to pass on an important message.'

Sam frowns. 'She did?'

Angelica's steps echo from behind, making my nerves jittery and flooding my veins with adrenaline.

'Yeah, she's having second thoughts,' I say, trying my best to keep my attention on Samuel and the job I have to do. 'In fact, she doesn't love you at all. Those were her exact words.'

'Tams,' Angelica says, from halfway down the stairs. 'What are you doing here?'

I glare at her. 'Sam and I are having a private conversation. Can you leave us alone please?'

Angelica looks at Samuel, who's gnawing on his bottom lip and gives her a look that says, 'I'll explain later', and she widens her eyes slightly in response. It makes my blood boil.

'Do you know that Sam is in love with Maz?' I say, anticipating that this bit of news will send her fleeing up the stairs and back to the house in tears.

Angelica's features soften into a smile. She's so beautiful I hate her.

'Yes. He told me just a few minutes ago. I'm okay with it. I think I've known for a while. Sam and I are close friends and we intend to stay that way. I'm happy for them.'

'Really? Maybe that's because you've got another guy named Cameron on the side.'

Angelica's face transforms from something beautiful into something hostile. She folds her arms across her chest. 'That is none of your business.'

'It is. Samuel is my business. And you've been screwing around behind his back.'

'I have not. Anyway,' says Angelica, 'I don't have to answer to you. Sam, let's go.'

Sam leaves his drink behind and heads for the stairs and I want to scream because this is all going horribly wrong.

Angelica extends her hand to him, but before he reaches for it, I rush up the stairs and push past him and give Angelica's hand a hard tug.

She screams and loses her footing and her eyes bulge as she sways then falls off the side of the staircase, her head hitting the cement with a crack.

Samuel and I are speechless as we watch the blood pool around Angelica's head.

'You killed her,' Sam says, his voice hoarse and strangled. He shuffles away from the blood, his mouth wide open in horror, his eyes red. 'You fucking killed her.'

A sob escapes his throat as he begins to pace the floor, his hands linked behind his head as he keeps repeating 'no' over and over again. Every time he looks at Angelica's bleeding head, fresh tears bloom in his eyes.

'Calm down, Samuel. It was an accident.' I go over to the table and quickly empty the blue sachet into his rum and cola, then stir it around with my index finger. 'Here, drink this and then we can go tell the others. They'll understand it was an accident. They're our friends.'

As he stares ahead into space he takes the drink but doesn't bring it to his lips. Tears spill down his cheeks and he whispers Angelica's name.

'She'll be okay. I bet it's just a concussion,' I lie. 'All that blood's just superficial. Now, drink this. It'll make you feel better. And then you can go see Maz.'

'I love Maz,' he says, his eyes glistening with emotion, before he takes one sip, then tips his head back and downs the whole lot.

'Good,' I say, rubbing circles into his back. 'So how are you feeling? Any different?'

Sam frowns and looks and me. 'What do you mean?'

'Have your feelings for me grown? Are you in love with me yet?'

Sam's eyes widen and he puts a hand to his throat.

'Tell me what you're feeling,' I say, unable to hide my excitement.

Samuel swallows thickly and makes a sound in his throat, his face turning red.

It's working. It's *working*. This is it. This is the moment Samuel confesses his undying love for me. I knew that white witch, Elora, from the internet was the real deal.

'Who do you love?' I ask, getting impatient now.

'I love...' He coughs, and his face is as red as the fresh blood pooling around Angelica's head. It almost seems as though he's choking. 'I love Maz... always... love Maz.'

Samuel grabs at his throat and looks at the stairs, but he coughs again.

'EpiPen,' he croaks, and I realise now, with horror, that the love potion powder must have had nuts in it. Shit. I should have checked the ingredients on the website before I ordered it.

I watch him struggle to breathe for a little bit longer, feeling strangely numb. Then he opens his mouth and I wait, hoping that by some miracle the potion is finally working. Then I can go get his EpiPen and we can finally be together.

But he brings his lips together and splutters, 'Maz...' before collapsing on the cold cement floor.

I stand there for a while, my heart broken, and then I step over Samuel, the boy who I thought was the love of my life, then race up the stairs.

The sea breeze is much stronger now, whipping my hair into a frenzy.

I close the hatch, kick off my ridiculous shoes, tossing them into the nearby bush, then run for the beach, hot tears building at the backs of my eyes – not because Sam is dying, or because Angelica is dead.

I cry because I'm unlovable.

And it's all Marilyn's fault.

34

Now

I must have dosed off, because I startle awake, my heart pounding in panic as I feel the rough surface of the tarpaulin against my skin and the cool sand in my ears. At first I think I must be dreaming, or even dead, but then I feel it… vibrations through the ground above me. Footsteps. Then, and I can't quite believe it, the slice of metal cutting through the soil above me.

I am being dug up.

Tamara was the one who knocked me out, and Lance wanted me buried. But Jake is the one who did the deed. Because while I was pretending to be passed out, I could hear Lance ordering him to do it.

The question is, what did they do to Jake after he buried me? Did Lance honour his threat and kill Jake so that he can pin all the murders on him?

My heart races as the vibration of the shovel slicing the earth gets closer.

If it's Lance digging me out, then there has to be a reason behind it. Maybe he noticed that I was still breathing while I was buried and had a change of heart.

No. I must be getting delirious from lack of oxygen. Lance isn't going to magically grow a conscience. Neither is Tamara. If I'm getting dug up, then it's not for a good reason. Maybe they buried me like this, with the tin on top so that they could easily dig me back up.

Threaten me to confess to killing Angelica and Samuel. If I refuse, then back into the hole I go to die alone.

Light streams in through the gaps of the tarpaulin and I swallow great gulps of fresh air, which hurts because my lungs had felt crushed only moments ago.

Sand trickles around my head and into my mouth. I cough and choke on it as I'm dragged by my feet from the tarpaulin wrap, and out of the shallow grave.

'That's it, cough it all up,' says Jake, rubbing my back as I retch and spit up as much sand as I can out of my throat. 'We need to move fast before they come back.'

The harsh light of day hurts my eyes making them water, and I rub at them while I catch my breath, hardly believing that I've been dug up. That I'm still alive.

'I'm not going to confess. I didn't kill anyone, Jake.'

Jake looks at me and tears off his eyepatch before tossing it aside.

'I know you didn't. After last night, I'm starting to think Tamara is the one who killed Angelica and Sam. And Lance killed the others. Now my own brother is setting me up. We need to get to the police before he does.'

He threads his fingers through mine and helps me to my feet. 'You okay to run?'

There's genuine concern in his voice and it makes me want to cry, but I swallow down any emotion and nod. 'I'm good.' I glance at the black eyepatch lying in the dirt.

'I don't need it anymore,' Jake says, before clearing his throat. 'Let's go.'

He moves quickly through the scrub and the bush, clutching my hand and gracefully and carefully dodging trees and large rocks. I start to gasp for breath as the terrain grows thicker and more difficult to move through. Jake notices and I'm grateful when he slows to a stop at a large fallen tree and gestures for me to rest against the log.

'Don't be afraid to tell me to stop if it's too much. I mean, you've only just been buried alive and all.' He grimaces at me, and I can see the remorse darkening his eyes.

'You put the metal sheet on top so I'd survive. You were planning on saving me.'

Jake sits down beside me.

'Yeah. I've suspected something's been off about Tams for a while. When we first met at the white house – that's what we called the psychiatric hospital – she would hardly look at me. No girls ever did. Maybe it was the patch, who knows? But after we had to break into pairs and tell each other about ourselves, well, I told her about my older brother and how he had big money coming when the police solved the case of who murdered his sister.'

I shake my head. 'Angelica.'

'Yeah. So she's suddenly interested in me and... it was nice.' Jake glances at me and looks away, his cheeks tinting pink. 'She kind of looks like you.' He shakes his head. 'But now I know why. It's all about that fella Samuel. She'll never love me. She'll never love Lance either. She's too crazy to truly love anyone, doesn't even know the meaning of the word. I reckon she gets a kick out of taking your man. While you were in the hole, she told me that she's been seeing him for months.'

I think about the 'gaming' friend that Lance had an affair with. Could that have been Tamara? But what about Sienna and the perfume? That part doesn't make sense.

I tell him about the perfume I smelt on Lance, the same one Sienna was wearing.

Jake nods. 'Tamara's handiwork. She sprayed Sienna with it yesterday. I couldn't understand why, but now I know. She was setting the poor girl up.'

My chest tightens as I think about Sienna. Maybe if I hadn't jumped to conclusions she'd still be alive.

Leaves crackle in the distance somewhere behind us.

'Shit. Let's move.' Jake takes my hand and tugs me along.

I have to leap over small bushes and dodge fallen branches to keep up, but the fear of Tamara and Lance catching up to us spurs me on.

After several minutes, Jake slows down again. 'I think we've lost them for the time being,' he says between huge gulps of breath, his arm resting against the rough bark of an old tree. 'Lance thinks he's smarter than me, my parents always thought that too.' His eyes film over with sadness and he looks away. 'But they locked away the wrong son. They'd be alive today if they'd locked up Lance instead of me.'

'Wait, what are you saying?' I ask, wiping the sweat from my brow with the end of my shirtsleeve.

Jake meets my gaze and shakes his head. 'Trust me, you don't want to know.'

'Lance was my boyfriend for over a year. I think I deserve to know.'

'Fair enough.' Jake shrugs lightly. 'Lance always had it in for our parents. He was always giving them grief. I guess I was a handful too when I was first adopted but I grew to love my parents, even if they sent me to the white house for a few months. They were worried about me. I'd been getting bullied at school and started wearing the patch in a bid to ward off the bullies. It strangely worked. But the patch bothered my parents enough for them to send me away.' He shrugs. 'I knew that if I ripped it off I wouldn't have to go away, but I just couldn't bear to give it up. I felt as though something bad would happen if I removed it.'

'What happened to your parents?' I ask.

'Lance happened to them.' Jake stares off into the distance, his blue eyes darkening. 'He always used to tell me that cutting the brakes on our dad's car would be the best way to kill our parents if we ever got sick of them. I used to nod my head and agree, but only because he was my older brother and I looked up to him.' Jake shakes his head and his blue eyes shine with emotion. 'I never imagined that he'd actually do it. The police said their brakes failed because they were faulty. But I know the truth.'

'Why didn't you tell the police?'

'Because I was young, and after it happened, I only had Lance, and he promised me money in the future, and a life of luxury living in a mansion in Bali – which sounds so stupid now. So I kept my mouth shut.' Jake rubs his eyes and clears his throat.

My blood turns to ice. So I've been living with a cold-blooded killer for over a year.

'Now I know why my car wouldn't start yesterday.'

'Yeah. Lance's handiwork. He needed a reason to come on the trip with you because he hadn't planned on you breaking up with him beforehand. Every moment he spent with you was leading up to this one weekend. Tamara promised him a confession. Nothing was going to stop him from getting what he wanted.'

I think back to the day I first met Lance, how he'd dined at my restaurant and sat there staring at me the entire time, a flirtatious smile on his lips. By the time he ordered dessert we had made a date to see each other again. Now I know that none of it was real. The hugs, the kisses, the tender words, the sex… all of it was fake. He only sought me out because Tamara told him that I'd killed his sister.

A twig snaps from somewhere behind us and a bird bursts out of the tree Jake is leaning against and flies away.

He squeezes my hand.

'Stay close,' he mutters beneath his breath. 'I'll do my best to protect you.'

'Surprise!'

Tamara and Lance spring out from behind a large shrub. Sunlight glints through the trees, reflecting against the long, silvery blade in Lance's hand.

As they move closer, I notice the blood that stains the knife, as well as Lance's fingers.

Lizzie…

'Give her up, Jakey boy.'

Jake holds fast to my hand.

'No. We're going to the police. If you kill us both, then you'll have nobody to pin all this on. You'll both go to jail and rot.'

Tamara snatches the knife from Lance's hand. Then everything happens so quickly it's a blur.

She screams and lunges at us, knife raised and glinting, but she trips and falls. Jake pulls me aside and tries to drag me out of Tamara's path and for a second, when I see Tamara on the floor, her eyes wide in shock, I think we're okay.

But then I look at the knife and see the fresh blood trickling down its sharp tip.

'Wait,' I say. 'Did she get you?'

Jake's eyes are wide as he shakes his head. I follow his gaze to my shoulder and gasp when I see the blood oozing out of me.

The pain, when it finally comes, is excruciating and sucks the air from my lungs, making me dizzy.

Jake's shadow moves over the sunlight as he hovers over me.

'You're gonna be okay, Maz,' he says, squeezing my hand. 'Just hold on.'

Jake's face begins to blur… then I blink and see Samuel gazing down at me, his eyes shining with love.

'Samuel,' I whisper, reaching for him with my good arm.

The forest above his head begins to blur and swirl, before everything fades to black.

35

When I come to, I'm flaked out on the ground and the bush around me is alive with the buzz of cicadas.

Tamara paces the dirt beside me, kicking up a miniature cloud of dust that coats my face and stings my eyes every time she takes a turn.

My heart drums a furious beat as everything that happened in the past twenty-four hours comes back to me, making the wound in my shoulder throb and my head light.

Tamara pauses mid-step and bends over to stare down at me, her eyes fixing on my bleeding shoulder.

'That's it, Maz, bleed yourself to death.' She grins, demonstrating just how insane she is. The idea of dying out here, Tamara the witness to my last breath, leaves me cold.

'Where's Jake?' I ask, hopeful that he has managed to run for help.

In that exact moment, someone, a man, screams. His piercing shriek sends all the birds from the nearby branches into a fluttering panic. I watch them flee high above the trees into the bright blue sky, wishing I had wings.

Tamara shrugs. 'There you go. Did you hear that? You asked a question, and Jake answered.'

'What are you doing to him?' My wound throbs more painfully as my heart works harder. I take a deep breath and gaze up at the perfectly clear sky through the canopy of trees. I need to calm down before I bleed out.

Something catches my eyes, flickering in the sunlight that streams through the tree branches as it falls gracefully, floating gently towards the ground. A feather, dark green with a little bit of blue and grey. It settles on the dirt to my right and using my good arm, I reach out and touch it with my fingertips. A wave of calm washes over me and the ache in my shoulder eases somewhat.

'Me? Lance is the one who's got him. My man – yep, you hear that, Maz? – *my* man is cruel so I'd say Jake's in a lot of pain right now. You know I stole Lance from you. He took one look at me and said, I want her. I want Tams.'

I stroke the feather some more and try not to think about what Tamara is saying about Lance being cruel to Jake. Poor Jake. He finally finds the courage to stand up to his brother and now this.

Tamara runs her hands over her now voluptuous figure and flicks her long dark hair over her shoulders. 'He didn't want you, he wanted me all along. How does it feel? To have the guy you love want someone else?'

'I don't love Lance. I never did. You already took away the one man I loved.' I gently rub the soft feather between my fingers as my eyes burn with unshed tears. 'Jake told me he thinks you killed Samuel. I'll never forgive you for it. For taking away my best friend.'

Tamara looms over me, raises her foot and brings it down against my wounded shoulder. I cry out, the excruciating pain shooting through my entire body. I'm going to die out here, at the hands of Tamara, the girl who I thought was my friend. The girl who killed Angelica and Samuel.

Suddenly a voice rings out close by. 'Police! Raise your hands!'

Tamara's face turns white. She does what she is told.

I attempt to raise my head but the forest around me spins.

Footsteps… everywhere. Running, trampling the shrubs and the grass.

Tamara screams and when I turn my head and blink, I can see that she is being cuffed.

Kind faces peer down at me, their eyes softened with empathy.

'She's the killer!' Tamara shrieks, spit flying from her lips as she glares at me. She struggles against the cuffs. 'Take these off me. Marilyn killed Angelica and Samuel. She killed them. Ten years ago. She's a killer.'

'No. She didn't.'

I move my head to the sound of the familiar voice.

'Lizzie? Is that you?'

The officers shush me and stroke my forehead. Someone is pressing something cold against my shoulder.

'Maz, I'm here,' Lizzie says.

I raise my head a little and I can see my friend's pale face, her arms streaked with blood. 'Tamara cut me. She tried to make it look like suicide…'

Lizzie drops from my view and I hear a thud.

'What happened to her?'

Some of the officers tending to me rush to Lizzie, one staying by my side, holding my hand.

'It's okay. She's getting help.' The officer smiles down at me but I can see the concern lining her forehead.

'Lizzie. Are you okay?' a man asks. It's a voice I recognise.

'Will? Is that you, Will?'

After a few seconds, a familiar face hovers over me.

'Will. Is it you that saved us?'

He crouches beside me and lightly touches my arm. 'It's going to be okay. The police are here now. You're all going to be okay.'

'Did you call them?'

He nods. 'Yes. Now shush. You need to rest and get better.' He leaves me, I assume, to tend to Lizzie.

I squeeze the officer's hand.

'Jake! You need to find Jake. Lance was hurting him,' I say. 'He was hurting him. You need to find him, please.'

'Oh, you mean this fellow?' The officer glances over her shoulder and nods, and although there's a seriousness to her expression, I can tell that she is all heart.

The next minute, Jake's face comes into view, along with the faces of the two officers who stand on either side of him, gripping one arm each. His skin shines with sweat and he has a thin cut across his throat that is red but doesn't appear to be bleeding fresh blood. Despite this wound, and the sheer terror he must have felt at the moment of infliction, he appears to be okay.

'Did Lance do that to you?'

'Don't worry about me. You get better, you hear? I'll come see you when I'm out.'

'Wait. What do you mean by out?' I try to sit up and feel a wave of nausea cloud my head and rise up my throat. 'Are... you in cuffs? Why is he in cuffs?'

'Shh, you're working yourself up. It's not good for the wound. We need to stop the bleeding,' warns the officer, frowning at me now.

'Don't arrest him,' I say, remembering the secure feeling of my fingers within his grip and the kindness in his eyes. 'This man saved my life.'

'They're just doing their job, Marilyn.' Jake stares down at me, a gentle smile on his lips. 'I've got to go now. You just concentrate on getting better.'

'Wait. I want you to have this.' I raise my good arm and offer Jake the feather.

He stares down at it and blinks several times.

The officer beside me plucks it out of my hand.

'Put it in my hands, please,' Jake says, his voice gravelly and choked with emotion.

Then they take him away.

Epilogue

It's been six months since that weekend away at the holiday house and I can say, for the first time in my life, that I'm feeling good. Happy. I'm actually enjoying life for the first time in a long time. Not to say that I don't have my glum days, the days I remember whom I've lost, the days I remember that we humans can be terrible people who thrive on hurting one another.

Tamara and Lance will both be locked away for a very long time. Tamara has been writing me letters. I now know exactly what happened to Angelica and Samuel and although I feel sick every time I think about it, I'm also glad that I finally know the truth.

But anyway, Tamara's letters will be returned to sender from now on because I've packed up my old life and have managed to fit everything in a nice little convenient backpack for the time being.

Before I started on my travels around Europe, I visited Jake in jail. He's doing time for his part in luring Sienna and Lucas into Lance's evil hands, but the fact that he helped me and tried to do his best to right the situation, helped the judge to be lenient on him. Jake plans on turning his life around once he's out of jail. He wants to work with troubled teens and help kids who are in the system like he was. He told me that if he can prevent any kids from going through what he did then he feels as though he has a purpose.

Lizzie and I, the only two left in our group, have finally made peace with each other. I've forgiven her for hiring Will. But it was easy to forgive her, because I know that Tamara had manipulated Lizzie into doing things she didn't want to do. Lizzie gifted Will a large chunk of money, enough so that he could quit being a male escort for a living and focus on his ailing father's health.

For the first few weeks after everything happened, Lizzie invited me to stay at her flower farm until I recovered from my injuries. It was a beautiful place to recover, surrounded by sweet-smelling roses among other beautiful flowers. Waking up each morning to enjoy my coffee out on the veranda and gazing out at row upon row of flowers was healing.

But, after I felt strong enough, I returned to my house, the house I shared with Lance, my mother's home that she left to me. It took only a month to sell once I put it on the market, and the lightness I felt, when I managed to squeeze what was important to me into one little backpack, was liberating.

Then I booked a one-way ticket to London and began my travels around Europe – yes, a big cliché, the Australian backpacking around Europe, but it's something my mother hoped I'd do one day. Samuel and I used to talk about it too, about our plans to visit all the places we'd dreamed about. So here I am, my feet in the glistening, clear waters of the Adriatic, on the beautiful, pebbled beach of Pupnatska Luka.

I raise my face to the warm sun and picture my mother and Samuel gazing down at me with soft smiles on their faces, before I wade into the cool sea and dive in. Beneath the surface I watch the fish wriggle past me and admire a beautiful bright orange starfish clinging to a large, smooth rock.

When I break the surface, I inhale the fresh sea air and smile.

Maybe I'll stay in the nearby village for a while.

There's no rush for me to return home. I don't have to waitress to support Lance anymore, and the money from the sale of Mum's house is enough to keep me going for a while until I decide what to do with my life.

But until then, as the locals say around here, when they drink a shot of rakija, their homemade spirit, '*Živjeli!*'

Let's live.

The End

If you enjoyed this book, please let others know by leaving a quick review on Amazon. Also, if you spot anything untoward in the paperback, get in touch. We strive for the best quality and appreciate reader feedback.

editor@thebookfolks.com

Also by Vanessa Garbin

WHAT WE DID LAST NIGHT

When a group of close friends decide to hold a partner-swapping key party one night, it is meant to be "just a bit of fun". No obligations, but no strings attached. And anything that does happen will remain under wraps. But things quickly start to unravel, with utterly deadly consequences.

THE LIES I TOLD HIM

When Daphne's teenage son returns from a party, distraught, he refuses to tell his mother what's up. But someone has filmed him in a compromising situation with a girl, and they are using it to get what they want. As Daphne tries to solve the problem, her own past comes back to haunt her and place everything she holds dear in jeopardy.

YOUR EVERY MOVE

When young mother Dana discovers a bag of money under a bush, she thinks her problems may be over. Unfortunately, they are only just beginning. She starts to receive letters from someone claiming to be her "number one fan" and unless she complies with their bizarre demands, her family will be in danger.

THE STEPS WE TAKE

A mother becomes increasingly at odds with her local community when she tries to deal with the bullying of her daughter at school. Yet her daughter is trying to handle it in her own way. When one bullying schoolboy goes missing, the family will have to reach the truth to remain together.

THEIR LITTLE SECRETS

Sara's marriage is already under strain when her best friend's daughter disappears. With the parents acting strange, and her husband absent-minded and evasive, Sara starts suspecting they share a secret. When the body of a girl is found in a lake nearby, her resolve to solve the mystery will force her to question everyone she thought she knew.

All FREE with Kindle Unlimited and available in paperback!

Other titles of interest

DEAD SET ON MURDER by Iain Henn

Eighteen years after disappearing without a trace, Jennifer's husband's body turns up, yards from her home. Apparently without aging one bit. She knows something is seriously amiss. Fortunately homicide detective Neil Lachlan shares her concerns. But when the case overlaps with a manhunt for a serial killer, it will put Jennifer's life on the line.

FREE with Kindle Unlimited and available in paperback!

THE NEWLYWED by Anna Willett

When newlywed Jane Wilson disappeared years ago, her husband fell under suspicion. But the police had no evidence. Examining the cold case, Detective Pope has a hunch that Jane was witness to a serious crime. Something dragged her back to the scene and made sure she'd never leave. And whatever that was, may well be alive and ready to act again.

FREE with Kindle Unlimited and available in paperback!

Printed in Great Britain
by Amazon

18371080R00123